BUCHANAN'S GAMBLE

BUCHANAN'S GAMBLE

Jonas Ward

A FAWCETT GOLD MEDAL BOOK

Fawcett Publications, Inc., Greenwich, Conn.

BUCHANAN'S GAMBLE

Printed in the United States of America
January 1973

Chapter One

Buchanan stalked into the Palace Hotel in San Francisco, towering above all the men. The women stared, smiled, and sighed. He wore trail-soiled range clothes and high-heeled boots. He carried packages under one arm. He was smiling, pleased with himself and the world.

Close on his heels came Coco Bean. He was almost as tall and possibly wider than Buchanan. He was black and the muscles bulged beneath his hickory shirt. He also was toting a large package.

Behind these two was a smaller man with both arms loaded with bundles. He wore an alpaca suit and steel-rimmed eyeglasses and had an air of unease.

The desk clerk stared. His sideburns fluttered. He had puffy cheeks and half-rotted teeth.

Buchanan said, "I want two rooms side by side. Got to have baths, too, if you got 'em in this fancy joint."

"Two rooms? For whom, may I ask, sir?"

"For me, Tom Buchanan. And for my friend, here, Coco Bean."

The clerk gasped. "For . . . for a nigra? Are you demented, sir?"

Buchanan placed his packages carefully upon the desk. He pushed back his hat. He looked around at those who were watching and waiting. His voice resounded in the lobby.

"I'm a peaceable man. Last thing I need is a fuss. I got a pocket full of money. I want a room for me and a room for Coco Bean—who is *not* a nigra. He is a black man who is the world champion fighter, that is who he is. Now rustle up some keys and leave us get to our business."

"We have a rule here, sir. . . ."

"I just broke it." Buchanan leaned a bit further, taking gold pieces from his pocket. "You see these? They buy what we need. Now hop to it, sonny."

The clerk looked into the blue-green eyes which had narrowed upon him, fixing him. People were crowding in, forming an interested circle.

Coco said, "If they don't want us, let's buy the place and fire ev'body."

The clerk gulped. "Uh, champion, did you say, sir?"

"World champion prizefighter, is what I said. And you're holdin' up Mr. Brame, here, too."

The man in the alpaca suit said, "No trouble at all. Not any, Mr. Buchanan, sir."

"Mr. Brame ain't got too much left to sell," Coco said. "We done bought him out."

The clerk reached for a pen, his hand shaking. "If you will sign the register?" He ducked and ran into an office at the corner of the desk.

Buchanan signed his name, then bit the end of the pen, He was from no place, from every place. For the first time in years he was having expensive fun. Finally he decided to give the address of his big black horse, Nightshade. He wrote, "Care of Joe D. Teller, Culebra, New Mexico." He started to hand the pen to Coco, remembered, and filled out the other lines for his companion.

It had been a long ride, starting the other side of the Black Range where he had acquired a small fortune in gold, finally descending into Culebra, his leg aching from a bullet wound, the most recent of many. Coco had been a nuisance because the black fighter was ever anxious that Buchanan should heal and regain full use of the leg, so that they might fight to see who was the better man. Since Buchanan never would indulge in fisticuffs for anything less than a cause, this created an awkward situation.

At this moment, however, Coco was entranced with the contents of the bundles from Sol Brame & Son, men's clothiers. He was further calmed by the knowledge that San Francisco was a town which nurtured pugilists, if not pugilism—there being a local ordinance against same. Coco was, in fact, biding his time as Buchanan well knew.

A man came close from the crowd. He was a burly man

6

in a bowler hat, a checkered suit, heavy gold chain swinging across well-filled vest. His nose bulged, his jaw protruded.

"Heard you say prizefighter. Coco? When did he win the world champeenship?"

"Can't say as I know who you are," responded Buchanan loftily. "If you're from the newspaper, I might talk to you."

"Name of Tim Cook. So happens I manage Jasper Krag. Also manage Joe Konecke, the Western heavyweight champion. Maybe we can do some business together."

"Look me up this evenin'," said Buchanan loftily. "We got some other offers."

"You won't get no place without fightin' Konecke," said Cook. "No place at all. I'm the man to see."

The clerk had returned to his place. He was reaching for keys.

Buchanan said, "Like I told you, Mr. Cook, see me this evenin'. Good day, sir."

They followed a uniformed boy to an iron cage. Coco shied, but the boy was so matter of fact and young Brame was so close behind that he entered, shivering. The boy pulled on a rope and the cage began to ascend.

Coco mumbled, "Rooms that go up into the sky, it ain't right, Lord. But you're on my side, Lord, and I can't get off, you can see that. So you gotta stay with me, Lord, stay with me."

The cage stopped. The boy pulled back the barrier. Coco stumbled into the hallway, still clutching at his packages.

Buchanan said, "Just stick with me and you'll wear diamonds, Coco."

"Diamonds ain't no good to a corpse." But Coco managed to make it to the door unlocked by the bellman, stepped inside, and rolled his eyes. "Man, this here is scrumptious. Purely scrumptious."

Buchanan went to the room next door, gave the bellman a dollar, and waved young Brame inside. It was a spacious room with deep, comfortable chairs, a wide bed beneath a white coverlet, billowy drapes at the long, tall

7

windows. It was scrumptious, all right. He had never been in a more scrumptious room.

He said to young Brame, "This ain't a bad joint, at that. Put down the bundles, there, and tell me somethin'. Who is that Mr. Cook was talkin' to me?"

"A sporting man, sir." Brame rubbed the circulation back into numbed arms. "A gambler. Prizefighting is illegal but the sports all promote it where the law can't find them. Or the law—well, you know, Mr. Buchanan, the law can be bought at times."

"I have known of such." Buchanan debated. "Is Cook a square shooter?"

"Well, sir, he's alive. Not that he wouldn't take advantage."

"I expect that's good enough. Now, about this Joe Konecke?"

"A very fine fighter. Maybe the best. Not so big, not as big as your man. But quick and durable. They say you can't knock him out with a crowbar."

"Good."

"Good, sir?"

"Uh—well, Coco is tougher than a boot. We need a good man to see just how tough Coco is, understand?"

"Oh, I see. I'll have to put a few dollars on Coco. If you make the match."

"Seems to me you know a lot about the game, son."

Young Brame flushed. "Don't tell papa, please. I do follow the sport a bit."

"And other sports?"

"Well, yes, sir. I do." He grinned. "Win a few, lose a few. I try to keep up."

"No harm in it. Sport is healthy. A man tailors all day, he's got a right."

"Thank you, Mr. Buchanan. Can I help you try on the garments, sir?"

"Help me? Why, I been dressin' myself since I was a week old," Buchanan said. "Just run along. I'll let you know about the fight if it comes off."

"Thank you, sir. I wish we had customers like you two every day." He bowed himself out.

Buchanan said to the closed door, "I bet you wish you

had suckers like me once a week. Even once a month, maybe."

Still, he had not bought himself decent clothing for a couple of years. He had been on the range, into scrapes, up in the mines, out with the cattle. He had been in jail in El Paso, which was where he had met Coco.

In fact it was in the El Paso hoosegow that he had thrown Coco clean through a window after a skirmish, leaving the superiority of one or the other undecided. He had felt the strength of the black man, and he had come to regard him very highly. It didn't matter to Buchanan who was the best fistfighter. Coco was a clean and decent man, scared to death of guns but willing to rush them for a friend. It was kind of a shame to tool him here and get him into prizefighting again just as a means of escaping him.

It was for Coco's own good. Buchanan had every belief that no pugilist could stand up to him. There was big money in the game if a man could get established, get backers to put up purses and to bet on him. Buchanan had known a good bit about it since his youth. He might indeed have become a champion himself except for the peaceable streak which was foremost in his character.

He found a sign saying that a bath could be had at the end of the hall. He knocked on the connecting door and called to Coco, announcing the fact. He undressed and wrapped a huge new robe about his enormous physique, took towels and soap, and went prowling. He found the bath and locked the door. He suddenly remembered he was in the big city and unlocked the door. He ran back to his room. He picked up his money belt, heavy with gold pieces, several thousands of dollars' worth, and carried it with him to the bathroom, where he shaved and bathed in happy peace for a half hour.

He dried himself and went back down the hall. Coco was peeking through a crack in his door.

"Go take your bath," said Buchanan.

"I just been eyeballin' these duds," Coco said rapturously. "Man, I tell you. They is just plain scrumptious."

"Get clean, get dressed, and we'll show us off to San Francisco. This is a new town to me too, you know."

"You sure you got enough money?"

"I've got enough—and figure to make some more. So hustle up."

He went into his room. He put the money belt on a bureau and began undoing the bundles. He had purchased everything for the two of them, from head to toe, from the skin out. Last of all he hung up his range clothing. Brame had promised him the hotel would have it cleaned. He was careful of his dusty range hat; it was a Stetson, and scarcely shaped to his head, purchased in Culebra where he had stabled Nightshade with his friend Jody Teller. A man could buy a Stetson but it had to be broke like a mustang. It might not mean anything in Frisco but it was important back on the ranges to which he meant to return as soon as he had his fun.

He donned black lisle stockings and nankeen underwear. He put on a white shirt with a frilled front around the collar of which he tied a silken black tie. The trousers were tightfittting on his heavy, scarred legs. He took a look at his wound—it had long since mended but he had kept that secret from Coco.

He tucked the pants into shiny, comfortable walking boots. He shrugged into a three-quarter-length black coat with satin lapels and looked at himself in the mirror. He set a new, soft black hat smartly on his head and posed.

He said, "Buchanan . . . you're a *dude!*"

Then he remembered the money belt. He removed coins enough for present needs and wound the belt about his middle. Then he removed coat and hat and packed away the other garments he had bought from Brame & Son. There were striped trousers, two short jackets, changes of underwear, kerchiefs, socks, more than a man might need. He had, he confessed, indulged in an orgy of buying. Brame Sr. had been a great salesman—and money never had meant anything to Tom Buchanan. If he had it, he spent it. If he didn't have it, he could always find a job and earn it. His was the carefree life of the western man, the pioneer plainsman.

He certainly was not accustomed to large sums of money, which was why he was forever forgetting about the

10

money belt. He had come into this small fortune through an escapade involving two young people, several killers, a bad woman, and a placer mine east of the Black Range—and the death of an old friend.*

He had earned the gold but he had not sought it and perhaps deep within him he was uncomfortable with such a large amount. Sharing it with the indomitable Coco was fun. Ridding himself of Coco and his insatiable desire for combat with Buchanan was also a sort of game, albeit a rather serious game.

Coco interrupted his thoughts then, by knocking on the door and entering, a bit uncertain yet wonderfully proud. He stood a moment for Buchanan's inspection.

He was attired in a plaid coat which accentuated his enormous shoulders and fitted snugly to his hips. His shirt was cerise, with black stripes. His trousers, stove-pipe style, were striped gray and black. His boots were city style, vented with elastic, pointed toes. In his hand he carried a hard, round hat.

Buchanan said, "Y' know, I thought I was the dude. Coco, you are like the flowers of the field. You are plumb pretty!"

"You're funnin' me." But Coco was pleased.

"I wouldn't fun you for the world. When the citizens of this burg lay eyes on you they will know you are really and truly the champion."

"Leastways there's no guns that I see around here."

"No guns. You know I left mine in Culebra."

"It ain't your guns that scares me." He peered at Buchanan. "You sure are a dude. Reckon we're a couple o' dudes. When we gonna eat?"

"Right now," Buchanan told him.

They went into the hall. Buchanan paused at the elevator but Coco took his elbow in firm grasp and steered him away.

"Nobody can tell me any old room that moves is safe," he declared. "There's stairs right yonder."

"You never seem to remember I got a bad leg," said

* *Trap for Buchanan,* Fawcett Gold Medals Books 1972

Buchanan mendaciously. "I'd rather ride than walk any day."

"You ride. I hope you don't fall down, Buchanan. Because then I never would get the chance to whup you like I am gonna whup you." Coco started down the wide, winding marble stairway. Buchanan pulled the bell for the elevator. Coco was far from stupid, he ruminated. It would be wise to work fast, meet with that Mr. Cook, and arrange the fight. Somehow, during the excitement, there would be a way to escape and return to Culebra, from whence he could start roaming again. He had not seen nearly as much of the West as he wanted. He meant to see it all before he died.

By the time the elevator had risen and descended, Coco was the center of attention in the lobby of the hotel. A man with a pencil and a pad of paper was shooting questions at him like rapid fire.

Coco said, "Nobody has ever beat me yet. I have fought in Chicago, St. Louis, El Paso, lots of other places. I have fought white men and black. I am the champion."

"London Prize Ring rules, I expect?"

"You make the rules. I fight."

"The sports of San Francisco would like to know if you will meet anyone who challenges you?"

Buchanan interposed. "My man will meet anyone in the world, providing the purse is big enough."

"You're his manager?"

"I am. Tom Buchanan's the name."

"You look as though you had been a fighter yourself."

"Not me. I'm a peace-lovin' man. But I'm meeting with a Mr. Cook here and talkin' a match. You can tell that to the people."

"Cook, eh? You going to fight Krag or Konecke?"

"Whichever brings the most money."

"That would be Konecke." The reporter looked dubious. "Cook usually insists a fighter has to get past Krag first."

"Cook's got to deal with me," said Buchanan. "If Konecke is the best fighter that's who we want."

The reporter seemed satisfied that he had a story. He

put away his pad and pencil and said, "You may be sorry. Konecke's a great fighter, maybe the best."

"He's not the best until he beats Coco Bean." Buchanan beamed upon the crowd which had gathered, wealthy citizens in fine clothing, wearing diamonds and gold. "And I'm bettin' he can't do it."

A young man swayed forward. He was dressed in the height of foppery. He twisted a gold-headed cane and stroked a silky mustache. On his other arm languished a pretty young girl in a low-cut, sky blue gown more suitable for nighttime than noon.

"How much?" demanded the young man.

"Name your bet," Buchanan said. He was strange to big city ways but he had known gamblers and their tricks all his life.

"A hundred? Five hundred?"

Buchanan said, "A thousand?"

The young man suddenly gulped. "Uh—five hundred will do. That Konecke beats your man, if there is a fight."

Buchanan said, "Should we put up the money with the clerk? Have it placed in the hotel safe?"

The young man said, "Er—will a bank draft serve?"

"If it is certified."

"Sir, I am Samuel Dade. My father is part-owner of the National Bank of Culebra, New Mexico."

"I see. You happen to know Jody Teller?"

"Jody? You know Jody, the liveryman?" The youth was startled.

"Knowed him for a donkey's age," said Buchanan. "I reckon you're okay." He took out gold pieces and led the way to the desk.

The young lady stayed close, her eyes widening at the sight of gold coins. Coco stood apart, watching, listening. Dade produced a blank draft on his father's bank and filled it in. The clerk, no longer supercilious, put draft and coins into a heavy envelope, sealed it with blue wax and ceremoniously placed it in the big safe in the wall behind the desk.

Buchanan said, "We're about to eat somethin'. Would you all like to come along?"

The young man said, "Uh, no. Sorry . . . I mean, some other time, maybe."

Exuding the odor of alcohol and bay rum he took the rather reluctant young lady by the arm and steered her toward the door of the hotel. She looked back, flirted a kerchief at Buchanan, smiling. It was only then that he noticed her gold tooth. He turned to the clerk.

"You know that boy?"

"Yes, sir. He's stayed here before."

"His bank drafts are good?"

"Yes, sir. His father has been here also."

"He keeps peculiar company for a banker's son, don't he?"

The clerk coughed. "Mr. Dade enjoys a good time every so often."

"I see." Buchanan turned to Coco and winked. "Let's you and me eat some."

They went out of the hotel. The streets were filled with people and carriages and drays going back and forth, up and down. It was all new to Buchanan and Coco. They asked a passing stranger where they could find steaks and he named a place on Stockton Street. They found it with no difficulty. Buchanan limped into the restaurant.

Again they were met by an objection. This time it was a big one-eyed man with a ferocious mustache.

"No niggers in this here place," he stated.

Buchanan said, "I'm purely gettin' weary of that kinda talk. I'll tell you once, then we want food. This is Coco Bean, champion fighter of the world. Now show us a place to set down and eat."

The big man asked, "A prizefighter?"

"A champion."

"Will he fight Konecke?"

"That is what we're aimin' to do."

"Right this way," said the one-eyed man. "Jake, come and wait on these here folks. You bettin' on your man, Mister——?"

"Buchanan's the name. How much?"

"Not me. All I want is to see Joe Konecke beat." He looked Coco up and down. "Me, I'm bettin' on your boy."

They sat at the table. Buchanan said, "Things is pickin' up. Next you know, they'll be invitin' us to a gala."

"Wouldn't care to go," Coco said. "I got to start runnin'. I got to train some. I been on a mule and on stagecoaches and whatever."

"Eat," said Buchanan. "Then we'll talk about trainin'."

"You didn't have that bum leg, we could spar together."

"Oh, no you don't. Not me. I'm no fighter."

Coco said, "Y' know, for an honest man, Buchanan, you are the biggest liar in the whole world."

They ate steaks and eggs and potatoes and apple pie and ice cream. The waiter and the one-eyed proprietor could not believe what they saw. The afternoon went away with their eating.

Dusk fell on the lovely city of the hills and they sat in the lobby of the Palace Hotel and watched the people coming to dine, all dressed formally, wearing broadcloth and silk and jewelry galore. It was a glittering throng and Buchanan admired it.

"Coco said, "I been lots o' places and never seen nothin' like this. Lawdy, look at 'em!"

"Seems like folks hereabouts got nothin' to do but show off."

"Must be a fine way to live."

"It's pretty, all right. But give me a horse and a sky over me with the stars blinkin' down."

"You kinda crazy," observed Coco. "I always think so and now I know I'm right."

"Who's this comin' at us?"

"It wants somethin', I'll bet."

It was a small man with a sharp nose and squinting eyes. It wore a sweater and a short-billed cap pulled down over one ear. It looked like a fish out of water in the Palace.

"You Buchanan? That Coco Bean?" It had a whisper for a voice.

"That's right."

"Cook sent me. Yer to folley me."

"For what?" demanded Buchanan.

"For a meetin'. The game's agin the law, doncha know that?"

Buchanan said, "Well, maybe. You go on, we'll follow."

"Name of Spike," said the little man. He turned and seemed to slide out of the lobby.

Buchanan said, "Keep your eye open, Coco. I'm carryin' gold, remember."

"Wish I could forget it. Makes me plumb nervous."

They went into the street. The man called Spike was waiting on the corner. He moved quickly, like a spider. Buchanan almost forgot to limp, trying to keep him in view. The streets were straight but Spike turned corner after corner, until it was apparent to Buchanan, who relied upon his sense of direction to keep him alive on the plains or in the mountains, that they were making circles, but toward the darker section of the city.

"I don't cotton to this at all," said Coco. "How we know this bird's from Cook?"

"How do we know Cook wouldn't coldcock us for money?"

"You think we oughta quit and go back?"

Spike had stopped and was gesturing. They edged cautiously to where he waited. There was a dark alley at the end of which was a dim light.

Buchanan said, "Tell you what. You bring Cook out here."

"Yer to come in."

Coco took the man by the back of the neck and pinched. "You get Mr. Cook, you hear?"

The little man squealed. His hand flashed to his armpit. Buchanan reached out and took from him a derringer.

"Now, now. Coco hates guns," Buchanan remonstrated. "You could be hurt, showin' Coco a gun."

"Put that thing away," Coco said. "I'll rip him up for pullin' that on me."

Spike, still in Coco's grasp, squawked, "Hey, Cook! Hey, they're killin' me."

At the end of the alley the bulky figure of Cook appeared beneath the lamp. Crowding past him came a huge figure of a man who ran rapidly and easily toward the mouth of the alley.

16

"Leggo of Spike," he bellowed. "Who the hell do you think you are?"

Coco let go of Spike, spinning him toward Buchanan, who held him with one hand. Then he took one step and met the big fellow. He feinted with his left and threw a long, devasting right fist.

It landed on the man's jaw. He spun around twice. He banged against a brick wall. He bowed forward, slid to the ground, his legs straight out before him.

Buchanan carried Spike in one hand, the derringer in the other, going into the alley. Cook put his hands on his hips and shook his head. There were others in the doorway looking on.

Buchanan said, "This little fella pulled this little plaything. You better teach him manners, Mr. Cook."

"Get lost, Spike," said Cook. "And stay lost until I send for you."

"I want my gun!" Spike wailed.

"Gun? You call this a gun?" Buchanan laughed. "I figure on wearin' this for a watch charm."

"Beat it," Cook ordered. "You heard me."

Spike glowered, hesitated, then trotted out of the alley. Cook turned and waved a hand.

"No trouble in here, Mr. Buchanan. It's just we gotta keep things quiet, y' know? These are respectable people, and that's the way it's done here."

"What about him?" asked Buchanan, indicating the man still seated on the floor of the alley.

"Him? Oh, that's Krag. Spike's his brother."

"Krag, your fighter?"

"Yeah." Cook allowed himself a slight grin. "Looks like your man won't have to fight Krag. Looks like what the newspaper says is all correct. C'mon and meet Joe Konecke."

The room was behind a hardware store and was loaded with merchandise. Lanterns were hung to provide plenty of light. There were a dozen men present, half of them seemingly prosperous, the others rough-looking members of the pugilistic profession. The biggest and brawniest had a shaven bullet head and curled cauliflower ears and arms almost as long as Coco's.

"Joe Konecke," said Cook. "This here is Coco Bean, the challenger."

"Champion," said Buchanan firmly.

"Joe's the champ."

A smiling gentleman said, "I am Jabez Otto. Pleased to meet you fellas. We'll get the word around each man claims the championship. That'll stir the interest. Now, about the purse."

"You do get down to business, Mr. Otto," said Buchanan. "How much?"

"Two thousand, winner take all?" asked Otto.

"Okay," said Buchanan. "Now, about side bets."

"You want to bet on your man?"

"Another two thousand," said Buchanan.

"That can be arranged."

"And five thousand against ten that Coco knocks him out." Buchanan beamed upon the assemblage.

Otto whistled. The entire crowd looked impressed. Cook scowled. Konecke seemed disinterested.

Buchanan said, "Any time. We'll be at the Palace. Now tell me, where do we hold this fight?"

Otto grinned. "Best place yet. You know we have to avoid the law. Of course word gets around, they get to know. The thing is to find a place they don't have to raid. Give them a chance to close their eyes."

"And where would that be?"

"Mr. Bullwinkle, here, happens to own a large barge. Big enough to hold all the people we can invite with prospects of success. We hold the fight in San Francisco Bay."

Buchanan cocked his head to one side. "You sure this barge will hold a gang of people without sinkin'?"

"We're positive."

"Well, okay."

"Two weeks from today?"

Buchanan looked at Coco, who was staring at Konecke. Coco said, "Two weeks ain't enough time to train right. But this ain't no big deal."

Konecke had pale eyes. They flicked at Coco. He said, "You lookin' for it, black boy. You really lookin' for it."

"See?" Coco laughed. "Big mouth. Two weeks is plenty."

18

Buchanan said, "I got money posted with the clerk at the Palace. Okay to put up the rest with the hotel?"

"Excellent idea," said Otto. He looked at the others. "Satisfactory, gentlemen?"

All were agreed. Cook seemed willing to go along with any arrangements made by Mr. Otto. Konecke, after his one remark, seemed somnolent.

"By the way," Otto said, "we prefer to have our fighters wear skin gloves. Saves the knuckles, so the fights last longer."

"Don't make no mind to me," said Coco.

"London Prize Ring Rules, to the limit?"

"That's my game," said Coco. "Limit's when I knocks them cold."

There was a slight commotion at the door. Krag came into the storeroom, leaning on the diminutive form of his brother Spike. They went into the shadows beyond the lamps without speaking.

Coco said, "Like that, y'see?"

Cook said, "You won't find Joe as easy as Krag. You got a lot to learn, Bean. Two weeks, then."

Buchanan took the derringer from his pocket. He flipped it to Cook. "Give it back to your boy. Tell him to be more careful with us country folks. It's been a pleasure to do business with you gents. Now we'll say good evenin'."

"Good evening and good luck," said Otto.

Back on the street, Buchanan asked, "How did I do, Coco?"

"You did good."

"First time for me. Is that the way it's done?"

"Just about. Places and people is different. But it amounts to the same."

"What did you think about Konecke?"

"Big, strong. Dumb, maybe, but mighty powerful. He'll be real tough to hurt."

"Is that why you lit into him?"

"Don't hurt to put somethin' in a man's mind. If he's got a mind," said Coco. "I know I got to train hard for this one. You see that shaved head? Hard like a rock."

They went back to the hotel and ate another big meal. The food was so good that Buchanan decided to take a steak sandwich up to the room in case he awakened hungry. He preferred the open country but San Francisco did have its points, he admitted.

Alone in his room he debated with himself. He would leave money for Coco with the clerk no matter what happened. Win or lose, he would not leave the mighty black man stranded. If they won, Coco would be rich—until the next fight. At any rate, Buchanan would not have to hit his dark-skinned friend and possibly receive blows in return.

He sometimes wondered if Coco could really whip him in a fistfight. As quickly he dismissed the thought. He knew there was nothing to prove. He had no intention in the world of ever fighting unless he was forced into it and he always hoped that would not happen.

But it always did.

He thought about the young man from Culebra and wondered if Papa Dade knew about his son's activities in San Francisco. Culebra boasted only one bank, a going institution handling the payrolls, the receipts, the proceeds of mining, cattle and farming on the high plain in New Mexico. Profits must be awful high, he thought, to support young Sam in his sportive gambling and womanizing.

He thought about the arrangements he had made. Since prizefighting was illegal it seemed that he had acted in the only possible manner. Mr. Otto seemed legitimate. Mr. Cook was a crook, no doubt, but the businessmen who backed the sport should be able to keep order.

The best way to go was to depend on common sense, he always believed. He only wanted to launch Coco on a career with money in his pocket and get back to Culebra. It seemed little enough to ask. He was spending his capital and taking all the chances.

Thus far it had been fun. Buchanan had not enjoyed a vacation with fun in so long he figured he had it coming.

Accustomed to early hours he fell asleep. He wasn't hungry until dawn when the steak was cold but still edible.

Chapter Two

It was a clear day. The waters of San Francisco Bay rippled and sea gulls swooped. The barge was anchored a quarter mile off the docks. Small boats of all descriptions made their way toward the low-lying hulk.

Buchanan said, "Any lawman that had an eye in his head could see somethin' is goin' on."

Mr. Otto, wrapped in a long cloak, smiling, said, "Of course. But we've convinced them they don't have authority out yonder."

Coco wore long tights, a sash of red, white, and blue, soft leather shoes, and a long woolen overcoat to his ankles. Buchanan carried a blanket. In his pockets were several pairs of skintight leather gloves. He wore his range clothing, all cleaned and pressed.

Cook, Krag, the glowering Spike and the towering Konecke stood nearby in a group, awaiting transportation. It had been decided that the fighters and their backers go aboard last.

Buchanan called, "Cook."

"Whatcha want?" Cook was nervous. He had bet everything he had on the outcome, Buchanan knew. All of Buchanan's money was covered with the clerk at the Palace Hotel.

"I'd like to see the gloves Konecke's going to use."

"That's none of your business."

Mr. Otto said, "No, Cook. Buchanan's privilege. I have seen his. Smooth, unlined leather."

"Okay, you've seen 'em. I'm satisfied." Cook put a hand in his coat pocket. "You don't see ours."

Buchanan went a few paces forward. "Now, Mr. Cook. You want to be square, don't you?"

"You mind your business, I'll mind ours."

Buchanan reached out. Cook squirmed, but with all his bulk, he was helpless in Buchanan's grasp. The hand came out of the pocket. The gloves came into view.

They were rawhide, and were ribbed with stitched lines which could cut a face to ribbons, open body sores at a touch.

Buchanan said, "Okay. Then we'll borrow a pair of yours. Make it even and we don't mind."

"There ain't but one pair. These are it." Cook was triumphant.

"Then Konecke will wear these." Buchanan produced a pair of Coco's gloves.

"Ho! Joe couldn't get his fingers into them," Cook said. "I had his made special."

"Then we'll find a pair to fit him."

"Mr. Otto said, "But there's no time. The boats out there are coming for us now."

"I see." Buchanan brooded. Then he brightened. He made a quick grab. He wrenched away the rawhide gloves. He ran to water's edge and threw them as far as he could, out into the bay. They filled and sank. He said, "Sorry about gloves. Reckon we'll have to fight bare fisted after all."

Cook was purple. "That's crooked. You saw that, Otto. You saw what he did."

"It was an excellent idea," said Otto. "We'd prefer gloves, but we can manage without. Bare fists were good enough for Tom Figg."

"Also Molyneaux," Buchanan said. "He was black."

Cook said, "I got a notion to call it off."

"Do so. You'll forfeit your bets," Otto told him.

The boats were coming in close. Cook blustered. All through it Konecke did not change expression, Buchanan noted. The big fighter was certainly not a man to be unnerved by trifles. Coco had figured him out, he was tough, he would be hard to hurt and harder to bring down.

The Krags were whispering together. Buchanan wondered if Spike was carrying his little gun. It was becoming a trifle uncomfortable in the wind. Clouds began to run a race across the sun and the bay darkened. Coco moved his feet, and danced a jig to keep his circulation going.

A hansom drove up, varnished wheels flashing. Two figures descended in haste, Sam Dade and a smaller person in trousers. They paid off the cabby and ran to where the group awaited the boats.

"Are we too late?" Dade was short of breath. His companion wore a soft hat pulled down low over the nose.

"Might be room for you." Mr. Otto was disinterested. All were preoccupied with inner thoughts.

Buchanan squinted at the smaller newcomer. He caught the flash of a gold tooth. He eyed the width of the hips and the narrow shoulders. It was the girl, all right. Dade was sneaking her to the fight against all conventions.

Coco said, "The water's gettin' choppy. I got no likin' for choppy water."

"Take a deep breath. If you get seasick we'll go broke this mornin'," said Buchanan. Konecke, he thought, would not react to anything like rough water. It would take a meat ax to upset his equilibrium.

The boats came to the dock, skillfully brought broadside by husky oarsmen. Cook and his entourage climbed down short ladders and piled into the first. Buchanan watched the girl, grinning to himself. Dade was uncertain. Buchanan said, "Might as well go with us, Dade. More room in our boat."

"Thank you," said the young man from Culebra. He turned to his companion. Awkward in the unfamiliar garb, she started down the ladder. Buchanan reached out, took her under the arms and leaned down, placed her in the bow. She flashed him a grin of thanks and he winked at her. The others went aboard. The oarsmen flashed long blades, dipped, and pulled.

Buchanan squeezed in beside the girl. "You like fights?"

"I don't know," she whispered, trying to keep her voice from exposing her. "Never saw one."

"What's your name?"

She put her mouth close to his ear. "I know you're onto me. I'm Flo Dockerty. Sam's real nervous, didn't want me to go along."

"Sam may have been right. But stay close and I'll try to take care of you."

"I figured you would," she said. "Men. I know all about men."

"What you two whispering about?" demanded Sam Dade. He was sweating despite the cool breeze.

"The fight," said Buchanan. "Coco, you all right?"

"I'm just before turnin' white," said Coco. "Which would purely kill me."

"It's not that rough," Buchanan told him. "Don't look at the water. Look up at the sky."

"I don't see no golden stairway."

"Never mind thoughts of heaven. Think about Konecke."

The boats swept through a lane of little ships and came to the barge. It seemed to Buchanan that the crowd of spectators left scarcely enough room for a ring. He boosted the girl, Flo Dockerty, over the side and Coco went gratefully up behind her. The swell of the bay had subsided. Buchanan pulled himself up and watched the referee fuss with the loose ropes inside which the fight would take place. He was an expert in these matters. The posts had been attached to the deck with iron clamps, which seemed steady and strong enough. He looked at the sun and estimated its position in regard to corners. Sunlight in a fighter's eyes could blind him.

There were no corner stools. Pails had been provided, and sponges. On his person Buchanan had various salves and ointments to stop bleeding and heal cuts. Coco stood in ring center, jigging from one foot to the other. Konecke faced him surrounded by the Krag brothers and Cook. Mr. Otto brought the referee and introduced him.

"Captain Flagg, gentlemen, the best official in the West."

Flagg had sharp eyes, wide shoulders, graying hair. Under his arm, Buchanan was startled to see, was a holster in which nestled a .38 caliber Colt. The captain was taking no chances. Fight mobs were known to resent gambling losses in no uncertain terms.

Buchanan said, "He looks fine to me."

"You both know the rules?" Flagg's voice was sharp.

"London Prize Ring," said Buchanan. "No gouging, biting, or kicking. Rasslin's okay. When a man's down the round ends. One minute to come to mark. Fight to a finish."

"I'll accept a towel from the corner," said Flagg. "I'll disqualify a man for fouling."

"Wait now," objected Cook. "That only calls for takin' away points."

Flagg regarded him bleakly. "This is a fight to a finish. Points for what?"

"Well, if both men go down together."

"Don't talk nonsense to me, Mr. Cook. Bring your man to the taw at my command." He turned his back and walked to the ropes. He flipped a paddle, indicated the respective corners.

Cook said loudly, "Seems like we get no breaks from him."

Buchanan said just as loudly, "We don't need breaks, just a fair deal."

Cook glowered, then steered Konecke to his corner. Buchanan stood beside Coco. They had been unlucky, the sun shone directly into their eyes.

Buchanan said, "Circle when you go out."

"That ain't my style."

"Circle him and get the sun at your back."

"I go right at 'em."

Buchanan said, "Okay. I'll pick you up."

Captain Flagg said, "Time."

The crowd cheered. They were pressed close to the ropes on all sides. Buchanan felt them behind him as he knelt, his eyes on the action. The two men came to ring center. Flagg raised a hand, then dropped it. Mr. Otto held the watch. Sam Dade and the disguised girl knelt just off to Buchanan's right. The girl's eyes flashed, her fists were clenched, she was enjoying it. Buchanan wondered if she was rooting for Dade's bet on Konecke. He doubted it.

swinging with a wide left, cocking his right.

Cook and the bigger Krag were in the opposite corner as handlers. Buchanan looked for Spike Krag, saw him sneak his slight form in next to Dade and the girl.

The fighters squared off. For a moment they poised. Then Coco went forward, ignoring Buchanan's advice, avoiding the left, retreating to keep the sun in Coco's eyes. He drove a straight left into Coco's neck. He crossed a terrific right which Coco never saw.

Buchanan was in the ring almost as soon as Coco hit the hard deck of the barge. He picked up the fighter and carried him to the corner. He made a knee, propped Coco upon it, applied the sponge, took out smelling salts and waved them beneath the nose. It was awkward working alone, and he wished he had help.

Coco opened one eye and coughed. Buchanan put away the salts and said, "You like bein' knocked down?"

"What did he hit me with?"

"It was his fist," Buchanan told him. "He's not only tough, he's quick. Now will you box him?"

"I'll kill him," said Coco.

Around the ring men were waving money, offering odds

"It ain't necessary," Buchanan told him. "Just wallop him good."

Konecke moved, amazingly swift for a stolid big man, that Konecke would win. Out of the corner of his eye Buchanan could see the girl urging Dade to do something which the young man refused. He caught her eye and signaled to her. She began working her way along the ropes toward him.

Flagg called time and the gladiators went forth. Konecke did not waste time. He rushed, swinging both hands in hammer blows.

Coco went into his dance. On his toes he flitted this way and that, arching his body, bobbing his head, blocking punches with his forearms. The crowd booed this tactic, seeking blood in the manner of their kind.

The girl's head, hat pulled low, turned up at Buchanan's knee. Without removing his eyes from the action he asked her, "What were you tryin' to tell your man?"

"He's not my man and I was advising him to copper his bet."

"Why?"

"Coco came out strong, didn't he? I knew he would."

"How'd you know?"

"I know men," she said simply.

Buchanan reached into his pocket and took out the last of his money, a sheaf of bills. "Bet this. I'll split with you."

"Done and done!" she said. She did not return to the side of Sam Dade. She squirmed around and began making silent signals to bettors close by.

Buchanan concentrated on Konecke. The big man was slowing down the attack, trying to corner Coco, using a straight left and feinting with the right. Coco was regaining his full power. Cook yelled at Konecke, who shook his head, sparring.

Coco stopped running. He led with a straight left. He hooked off the jab and caught Konecke coming in. He threw the right from his hip. He connected with the cheekbone and Konecke went down as if shot, rolling over, bleeding. Now Cook and Krag rushed to their man, dragged him to the corner. He sat on Krag's knee while Cook worked on him.

Coco leaned against Buchanan's broad chest and said, "I opened him up. He bleeds good."

The girl asked, "Can I help?"

Buchanan said, "Reach into my pocket and give me the Vaseline."

She put it into his hand. He greased Coco's nose and brow. Coco got up and danced.

Flagg said, "Time."

They went to ring center. Coco flew to the attack, aiming for the gashed cheek. He again found the sun in his eye. He had left himself open. Konecke fetched him a ringing right that rolled him to ringside. His head went through the ropes.

Buchanan was on his way to the rescue when he saw Spike Krag make a swift, furtive motion. Coco's head jerked to one side. Buchanan bent down and saw a lump rising behind Coco's ear.

He stood up and spoke to Flagg. "I claim foul."

Flagg came and looked. He examined the swelling. "It must have happened when he hit the deck."

"It happened when he was hit with a blackjack," said Buchanan. "Search that man." He pointed to Spike.

Flagg said, "Come here, you."

Spike stood up, spread his arms. He smirked. "Search me. Go ahead."

There was no weapon on him. There was a ripple of movement in the crowd. Spike had passed the weapon on to confederates, of course, Buchanan reflected. It would be overboard in a jiffy. There was nothing to be done about it.

He returned attention to Coco with little hope that the fight would continue. The girl was there. She was rubbing Coco's neck with one hand, sponging him with the other. Buchanan hastily administered the smelling salts.

Coco grunted and came to his feet in one motion. "You can't tell me that ol' boy hit me in the ear."

"No. It was someone else."

"The referee?"

"Not him. Just go and knock out Konecke, please," said Buchanan. "You're gettin' careless. Right now I could whup you with one hand, bum leg or not."

Coco swelled like a bullfrog. "Don't you never believe it! Lemme at that baby!"

He flew out to the taw, stepped back, circled, then came in. Konecke took a terrific blow to the head and staggered back. Coco overran him. Konecke, dazed, retreated.

Buchanan said to the girl, "That was good work."

"It had to be done. I saw Spike slug him."

"I'll attend to Spike later."

"That's a bad bunch," she cautioned. "All of them."

"I'm a peaceable man but I can be a bad bunch, too." The thought of Coco being slugged in that manner riled him to his boots.

She said, "Coco, look out!"

Konecke was faking injury. He suddenly came to life, swinging for the head. Coco ducked, went in. He put a crossbuck on the tall man. He flung him hard. Konecke's head now bounced on the deck.

Coco was back in the corner. He said, "Doggone, sounded exactly like some lady called out to me. You think an angel come down them golden stairs?"

"No angel," said Buchanan. "Useful, but no angel."

People were staring, the few who had heard the distinctly feminine voice. Flo hid behind the bulk of Buchanan.

Coco said, "Me, I believe it was. It is a sign."

When time was called he went into a crouch. He circled again, got the sun at his back. He stuck out a fast left. Konecke was impaled upon it. Coco hung him on the punch, repeated it like beating a drum. Konecke reeled.

Coco went in. He lowered his sights and punched for the body. His fists went in like slung rocks. Konecke slowly folded over.

Coco threw the uppercut from his hip. He landed on the chin. Konecke's feet flew up. He went over on his back and described a somersault. A groan went up from his supporters as his seconds burst from the corner and hauled him away.

Coco stood and danced a little step, waiting. "He gets into it again, he never gonna live. He had it."

Flagg was watching Konecke's corner. He detected Cook reaching for the lighted cigar of an adherent, saw him apply it to Konecke's spine. He started forward. Konecke groaned. He did not awaken. Flagg walked to Otto, asked for a reading of the watch. Then he said very loudly, "Time."

Konecke's knees twitched. They tried to haul him to his feet. Flagg began to count, not too slowly. The crowd was howling to the skies.

Flo said to Buchanan, "You see that crowd behind Konecke's corner? Maybe a dozen of 'em?"

"I see them. Coco, watch them."

"That man can't come to the taw," muttered Coco. "I know he can't do it."

Flagg said, "Eight . . . nine . . . ten. . . . The winner is Coco Bean."

He was lifting Coco's hand when the fight broke out. The dozen with Cook and Krag were bunched together. Bettors were clamoring for their money. Fists began to fly.

Buchanan and Coco made a rush. They began knocking

first one, then the other of the bullies to the deck. Buchanan saw Spike Krag trying to duck away, caught him. He hoisted him high, then dashed him into the crowd. Men went down like tenpins.

Captain Flagg's stentorian voice cried, "Enough of that."

He stood with drawn pistol. Of a sudden no one moved.

"Pay off all bets," said Flagg. "Right now."

Flo was already busy collecting her winnings. Sam Dade made his way to her. She laughed at him. She came to Buchanan, counting the winnings. She gave him his share, pocketed the rest.

"Any time you're ready," she said. "Sam's mad at me."

"I'm not mad," Dade said. "I'm just broke."

The rowboats stood ready. Buchanan said, "Let's get out of here. My money's at the hotel."

Coco's admirers were hoisting him to their shoulders. Cook's crowd was tumbling into the other boat, loading it to the gunwales.

Flo asked, "What about the new champion?"

"He's happy. We'll see him later." He handed the girl and Sam Dade into the boat. It was quickly filled. The long oars plied and they headed for the dock.

Flo said, "I don't think I get it."

"Men were beginning to get onto you," Buchanan told her. "It could cause a riot. Dade, you were a fool to bring her."

"Me? Try and stop her." Dade was disconsolate. "Look, Buchanan, could you hold back that draft until I get back to Culebra?"

"Why, son," said Buchanan, "I'll go along with you."

"But I'm leaving right away, soon as I pay the hotel bill."

"You and me."

"Without Coco?"

"Coco's okay. He don't need me anymore." There was no use trying to tell the truth. It sounded silly.

"It doesn't seem right," Flo said. "There'll be a celebration and all that money. It doesn't seem right."

"I'm taking that stage," Sam said gloomily. "I got to."

"I'm with him," said Buchanan.

30

They landed and took a waiting cab. They dropped Flo at her boarding house, went on to the hotel. Buchanan went to the desk while Dade went up to fetch his baggage.

A strange man looked inquiringly at Buchanan. "Yes?"

"I'm Buchanan. Where's the other fella?"

"Oh, you mean Jones? He quit this morning. Took off without a word. Very strange."

Buchanan's stomach seemed very empty of a sudden. "Mind lookin' in the safe? Should be envelopes with money in them. Bets on the fight, y' know? They were all labeled proper."

"Oh, of course." The clerk worked the combination. There were no envelopes. The man investigated. He straightened and said, "The hotel cash is there, all straight. Jones didn't steal it."

"Yeah," said Buchanan dolefully. "He wouldn't. That'd be illegal. He got ten, twelve thousand dollars of bettin' money, which the police ain't interested in."

"I'm sorry, Mr. Buchanan."

"I'll take my bill and Coco Bean's." Thanks to Flo Dockerty, he had enough and some to spare.

He went up in the elevator and packed as quickly as he could. He came down carrying a bulging huge carpetbag. He went to the desk.

"Do me a favor. Tell Coco Bean that the bird flew off with our money. Tell him to keep all he won, the purse and all. Tell him I had to run."

"Run?"

"He'll know. But don't give a hint where I'm runnin' to. He'll think I'm after Mr. Jones."

"I don't understand but I'll do as you say."

"Thanks." Buchanan went to where the stagecoach waited. Sam Dade came hurrying behind him. They greeted each other without joy and clambered aboard. One other passenger was wrapped in a cloak, huddled in a corner, evidently already asleep. Buchanan told Dade nothing, he felt like such a fool. Trusting a stranger with all that money had been the dumbest thing he had ever pulled, he thought.

The driver came and snapped his long whip, six horses strained, and the stage rolled away from the hotel.

They were out of the city when the figure in the corner sat up and flashed a gold tooth. Flo Dockerty said, "Hi. You dudes think you were goin' to spend all that money without me?"

Dade moaned, "Oh, no. Not you. Not in Culebra."

Buchanan blinked once, then roared. His laughter shook the coach. The other two stared at him.

"Have you lost your mind?" demanded Dade. "My father will kill me, losing five hundred, and bringing her home."

"Too bad, I'm sorry for both of you. Y'see the hotel clerk ran off with all the money. And your note for five hundred, Dade."

Flo cried, "Jonesy? Jonesy did that?"

"You know the galoot?"

"He was a con man before he turned straight. A con man and an actor. No good at either job so he went to work in the hotel. I never thought . . . Jonesy, that bum!"

Buchanan said to Dade, "And she said she knew all about men. Goes to show you can't believe everything a woman tells you."

"I owe you the five hundred," said Dade morosely. "I wouldn't welch on a bet. But my old man . . . where he'll send me this time I couldn't guess."

The stage rolled on. It was a long way to Culebra. The passengers were silent, wrapped in their separate thoughts.

At the Palace Hotel the little man named Spike Krag questioned the new clerk. "We like owe Mr. Buchanan. A bet. Gotta have his forwardin' address, like."

"Why, let me see. He didn't leave one."

"Okay. Where'd he come from, then?"

"Let me look. Ah . . . yes. Culebra, New Mexico. Care of one Joe D. Teller."

"Couldja write it down for me?"

"Why certainly. Mr. Buchanan—er—suffered a loss. I'm sure he will be happy to receive money due him."

"Yeah. Uh—T'anks."

Spike scuttled out of the hotel. His brother and Tim Cook were waiting for him.

Chapter Three

Culebra was a large and busy town, the most important in that part of the high plain. There was only one bank but there were eight saloons, one of which, The Silver Dollar, was the center of social activity, providing gambling, dancing, and entertainment of a sort. Prosperity was the keynote of Culebra.

Joe D. Teller, known as Jody, was a lean man with a hatchet face, wide-spaced blue eyes, and a sharp nose. He owned the stage station and the livery stable and had an interest in mines. He employed two or three men to do the actual labor and contented himself with knowing everything that went on among his neighbors.

He said to Buchanan, "Nightshade needs work. He's fat and lazy. So they stole your stake, huh?"

"Like I told you." Buchanan couldn't care less. "Got a couple hundred left, enough for a stake."

"Funny thing, you comin' in with that new girl Rick Coverly hired over to the Silver Dollar. She sings pretty good. Kicks a nice leg, too."

"Flo Dockerty? Yeah. She knows about men."

"I bet she does."

"Not the way you mean. She's a smart one."

"They all are. She better look out for Addie Hale, y' know. Addie's Rick's gal."

"Addie'd better look out."

"And young Sam. Back from his foolishness. You met up with him, too."

"That's right."

"Everybody knows about him. Straight as string here to home. Wild as weeds when he gets away. His old man'll kill him some day."

"Could be." Buchanan had not cottoned to tight-faced old Daniel Dade. In fact he had refused to allow Sam to pay off the bank draft in his favor after he had seen the way Daniel treated his son. Some day he could return to Culebra and collect. Sam was grateful. He might need a young banker for a friend in the future.

"Reckon your black boy'll make a fortune now that he beat Konecke," Jody went on. "Konecke was reckoned some punkins in sportin' circles."

"Appears to me you know a heap about Frisco your own self. You and young Sam run together up there?"

Jody grinned. "It has been known to happen. Sam's okay. Just sowin' a few wild oats."

A tall young man wearing a badge on his vest walked into the yard. "Howdy, men."

"Howdy, Marshal Hagen," said Jody. "You pinched any drunks lately?"

"It's about all there is to pinch," said Hagen. He was a pleasant-looking young man, blond, handsome, a bit of a dude. He wore his gun tied low. "It's a tame town."

"That's the truth. The Silver Dollar's the only life we got. I don't know why we keep them deputies of yours on the job, cause we sure as blazes don't need 'em."

Hagen said, "Ask the selectmen. They ride shotgun for the bank and the mines is about all. I didn't hire 'em."

"My taxes pay 'em," said Jody. "However, things is good. Reckon old Dan'l Dade and the others need protection."

"Old Dan'l ain't the one. It's Walt Store more'n Dan'l."

"Walt's an ambitious man. We're lucky to have two bankers like Dade and Store."

"Reckon we are." The marshal looked at Nightshade. "That's some hoss you got there, Buchanan."

"He's a good un," Buchanan admitted. "Fat and sassy right now, but he'll be all right time I get over the range."

"You ridin' back over the Black Range?"

"Thought I might. Visit some friends."

"Come back soon, you hear?" The marshal walked on down toward the Silver Dollar.

"Now, there's a case," said Jody. "Poor Tim. He's got a case on Addie and Addie is head over heels for Rick."

34

"Do tell." Buchanan was weary of the gossip. He went to Nightshade and talked in his ear. The big black stallion nickered but his tail switched with impatience. "Well, thanks for takin' care of this one. Be seein' you, Jody."

"Have a good trip."

Buchanan put a foot in the stirrup. Nightshade did a gavotte to his right. Buchanan, expecting the move, swung up, tightening on the check rein. Nightshade went into a pirouette. Buchanan swung him for the street. Nightshade fishtailed once. Buchanan sat him tight and brought his head up, and the horse was off on a run.

Dogs and horses and people scattered. Nightshade ran like the wind. Culebra quickly vanished in the background. The trail went eastward and upward. Buchanan set the horse to it and slowed the pace. It was a fair morning, perfect for a ride. The saddle felt good beneath him, the horse solid between his knees.

The sun glittered on the rocky side of a ravine. There were no foothills in this section of the range, the trail went up and up toward the fleecy, fat clouds. All the colors of the rainbow were on parade. Nightshade settled down to a walk, lathered, the sweat running from him. Buchanan inhaled with pleasure, all the odors of the mountain familiar to his nostrils.

A fat little burro came around a bend in the trail and brayed, bracing all four furry legs, blocking the way. Buchanan laughed at the serious expression on the brindled face of the tiny beast. He dismounted and trailed the reins, going forward.

"So, little fella, you're plumb stubborn now, ain't you? This is your road and the hell with anybody else, right? Well, we'll just turn you around and see which way you go."

He was reaching for the burro when he saw the fresh big hole in the green brush which lined the road. He pulled back and walked to the edge of the ravine. Down below he saw trees bent under a falling solid force, saw a man's boot, saw the head of a prone horse.

He examined the terrain, talking to Nightshade, calming the black. The burro brayed again on a mournful note, then turned tail and went back around the bend of the trail.

There was a way down, working from handhold to tough root to treetop. Buchanan began the descent. Only a man of tremendous strength and balance could have made it. He was patient, taking no chances.

He came at last to the foot of a pine. The horse's neck was broken. The man lay clear. He was on his face, lifeless, clad in black town garments and city boots. Buchanan turned him over.

"My God, it's Dan'l Dade!" he said aloud. He squatted, looking closely at the body. There was a rip in the black coat. Buchanan looked up at the branches through which horse and rider had plunged. Then he examined the cloth. He shook his head. "If that wasn't done by a knife, I'm that burro's uncle," he said to himself.

He looked at the old man's face. It was pinched in death. The eyes were staring, baleful, he thought. There was a meanness about Daniel Dade which his demise had not softened. He seemed even yet to be calculating a profit for himself.

He had been a widower with only Sam for family, a son he had despised. According to Jody, his dealings had always been within the law but not always just. He and his younger partner, Walt Store, had foreclosed when they might have shown mercy. They were not popular in Culebra, they were respected only for their power.

Buchanan now went to the dead horse. Flies were already buzzing about its eyes. He shooed them away with his hat. There was a dent in the horse's head between the eyes. It looked as if it had been struck with something like the muzzle of a heavy gun.

Nothing was certain but Buchanan searched the clothing of Dade next, going through every pocket. He found only an old leather wallet with a few dollars in it. He looked then for saddlebags and found none.

There was no proof, but something was wrong. He knew something was wrong.

He walked in an ever-widening circle around the horse and the man. He examined each square foot of ground. He became certain that no one had been here before him. No one had followed the long fall to the dead animal, the dead man. Therefore if there had been foul play it had taken place on the narrow mountain trail above.

He began the climb. It was twice as difficult as the descent had been. While he struggled up the tree, to the face of the cliff his mind went over several possibilities.

If Daniel Dade had been murdered and shoved off the trail into the ravine to make the death appear accidental there had to be a reason. The man was a banker, therefore he could have been carrying a large sum of money. Also, he was a cold man with enemies. The motive may have been revenge. Then again, he may have been mixed up in some kind of a business deal which would harm another person and that person had taken this means to save himself.

Buchanan had seen a lot of killing in his time. Some of it had been senseless, committed in anger on the spur of the moment. Others were self-defense. Others were in battle. But murder, as such, he had always thought was done either for vengeance or for profit, unless it was from jealousy or pure hatred.

He came over the edge of the cliff to the road out of breath. Nightshade was cropping sage at the edge of the trail. Buchanan rested for a moment.

If he had good sense he would ride on. Daniel Dade meant nothing in his life, he had disliked the man on sight. The world would little miss him, his son would inherit and most likely sell out to Walt Store and move happily to San Francisco where he would either straighten out or spend himself into bankruptcy.

On the other hand, there was a dead man down among the flies. He had a decent burial coming to him. The marshal and the coroner would be involved . . . and all sorts of other people who had done business with him.

Buchanan mounted Nightshade and turned his head back down the steep trail toward Culebra. The day was no longer beautiful. There was a bad taste in Buchanan's mouth and an insistent inner feeling that he had come upon something very ugly indeed.

The funeral was over. Buchanan sat in the office of Marshal Tim Hagen.

"Terrible accident," Hagen said. "Could have been one of those wild little burros scared the horse. Could have been a snake—anything. Terrible."

Buchanan said, "The horse was a hack. Jody tells me nothin' would spook him. Dade was no horseman, he insisted on hirin' that animal when he rode, which was seldom."

"You keep gettin' at something," said the Marshal. He bit his lip. "Dr. Dudley said it could've been accidental."

"Dr. Dudley also said there were suspicious marks on both Dade and the nag."

"I know. I know." Hagen wiped his forehead with a blue bandanna. "Young Sam—well, I reckon you put the idea in his head."

Buchanan was puzzled. The lawman did not seem angry at his insistence that Dade might have been murdered. There was something on his mind but it was not resentment.

The door to the office opened and the two deputies entered. Dutch Hempel was a giant of a man with a scarred face. Sig Frey was short and thin. Both were heavily armed. Hempel carried a Bowie knife, a weapon seldom seen in that country. Frey was known to be a swift gunslinger.

"You still here, Buchanan?" Hempel's natural expression was a scowl.

"You see me," Buchanan said.

"Seems like you were in a big rush to get away the other day."

"Was I? Who told you that?"

"We know what goes on in Culebra. That's our job."

Marshal Hagen did not say anything. In the company of his deputies he was always silent, fading into the background as though they were in command. Yet he was their superior. It seemed odd.

"You wouldn't be hintin' that I'm not wanted around here, would you?"

Frey interposed. He was easy in manner, and smiled a

lot. "Course not. Dutch, he takes himself real serious. Don't pay him no heed. Nobody's roustin' you none."

"Thanks," said Buchanan. "Well, be seein' you boys."

He went out of the office. He walked across the street to the bank. Young Sam was in his father's office; with him was Walt Store.

Store was about forty, a well-turned-out man with cool, banker's eyes. He had been in Culebra five years. He had brought capital with him and invested wisely and with Daniel Dade had started the bank. Also with Dade, he had discouraged others who tried to get into the banking business, Jody Teller had said. It was Store who had insisted that Hempel and Frey be hired to ride shotgun.

Buchanan said, "Gettin' things straightened out okay?"

Sam was agitated. "We've just gone over our books. There's money missing."

"I don't think that's any concern to Mr. Buchanan," Store said quietly. "I don't think we should discuss it with anyone outside the bank."

"Buchanan thinks my father was murdered," said Sam. "If he was carrying all that money, then I believe it, too."

Store nodded. He made a steeple of his hands and peered at Buchanan. "I know your theory. And it may well be correct. But, you see, we don't know if Daniel was carrying the money."

"Fifty thousand dollars has just vanished," said Sam. "Cash money. Only two people had access to it. You and Dad."

"True. I assure you, I don't have it. But if Daniel was carrying it when he was killed, where was he going with it? What was he doing up on the trail? What was his motive in taking the money from the vault?"

Buchanan said, "You don't know of any answers? Any reason?"

"There was no deal pending for the bank which would involve such a move."

There was a silence. Sam twisted around in his chair. Store was impassive.

Buchanan said, "Looks like you got a mystery on your hands. Seems like the law should take a looksee into it."

"I've talked to Hagen. He just—well, he just shakes his

head and acts dumb," said Sam Dade. "I plain don't understand his attitude."

"Like someone told him to lay off?" asked Buchanan. "And he don't know whether to obey or not?"

"That's it. That's the impression I get."

"We have enemies," Store said thoughtfully. "All bankers have enemies. But I don't know anyone powerful enough to handle Hagen and his deputies. No, it doesn't seem possible."

"Yeah," said Buchanan. He arose. "Well, reckon I'll be gettin' along over the mountain. Jody must be gettin' tired of feedin' me. And I got the notion those deputies and maybe the marshal would like to see me go. I'll say so-long now. Be leavin' early in the morning."

He went down the busy street to the Silver Dollar. There were always a few customers in the place, miners off-shift, cowboys in town for supplies or just plain fun, citizens of Culebra pausing for a short one or two. It was afternoon and Buchanan did not expect to see Flo Dockerty, who worked at night.

She was at a table in the far rear of the place. Rick Coverly and Addie Hale sat with her. She beckoned to Buchanan.

Rick Coverly was almost too handsome to be real. He wore his hair rather long, his mustache was waxed. He had a straight nose, wide-spaced blue eyes and he was swarthy, with smooth skin free of blemishes.

Addie Hale was red-haired and lean. Freckles spiced her clear complexion. She was extremely pretty for a saloon girl, there was nothing hard or calculating about her appearance. She could scarcely ever take her eyes off Rick Coverly, whom she worshiped.

Buchanan sat down and Coverly moved a bottle within his reach, smiling. "On the house. You learn anything good?"

"Not a thing." Buchanan poured himself a drink.

"Somebody killed him," said Coverly without much interest.

"What makes you think so?"

40

"He had it coming. He was a no-good skinflint."

Flo Dockerty said, "I just got here and that's what I hear. We hear a lot, us girls, don't we Addie?"

"Not me. I don't hear nothin' like that."

"You don't listen, duck," Coverly told her. "Which is just as well. If there's a run on the bank we're all in trouble."

Buchanan asked, "Why should there be a run?"

"If someone killed Dade it means there's trouble. Some kinda trouble. You ask me, this town's settin' on a powder keg and the fuse is lit."

The saloonkeeper was positive in his belief. His position as owner of the principal bar gave him access to all the gossip, all the speculation among the males of the town. Buchanan nodded.

"There's a feelin' you get. Trouble and more trouble. Me, I don't care for trouble at all. I'll mosey along."

The bartender called, "Hey, Rick. Shipment's in."

Coverly said, "Good. We were runnin' low on booze. 'Scuse me while I go check the delivery." He got up, then looked at Buchanan. "Kinda wish you were stickin' around. You been here and there. I'd make a bet you've worn a badge in your time."

"You've got three lawmen."

"*You* can call 'em lawmen." Coverly shrugged and went to attend to the delivery of liquor. Addie followed. She followed him wherever he went, lingering in the background, ready to perform any small task that he might need attended to.

Flo said, "Not a brain in her head, but she sure loves that man."

"You've heard something."

"Uh-huh. Dade was carrying a lot of money."

"People are saying that?" It would start the run on the bank if it got noised around, he thought.

"Not people. Those deputies."

Buchanan's ears burned of a sudden. "Anybody else overhear 'em?"

"I don't think so. They were hittin' the bottle and I'd

just finished a number. I was behind the piano. They didn't see me. They seemed sorta happy about it. You know what I mean?"

"People didn't like Dade."

"No. Not like that. Just . . . happy."

Buchanan said, "Advice is worth what it costs—nothin'. But if I was you, I'd try another town about now."

"I didn't know you cared." She cocked an eye at him. "You get your five hundred from Sam?"

"No. Didn't ask for it."

"Well, you better had. Here's your chance."

Sam Dade was coming toward them. He was pale and shaken, but at the same time purposeful. He sat down, poured himself a drink, and without preamble addressed himself to Buchanan.

"I owe you five hundred. I'll double it if you'll stay and see this thing through."

"I'm no detective," said Buchanan. "Just happened I found your pa."

"You've got an opinion, though."

"Well, there was the rip in his coat. And no saddlebags. If he was carryin' fifty thousand he'd need saddlebags. And then the horse. There was a hole on his head."

"You figure somebody robbed him, then ran him over the side of the cliff?"

"It sure looks that way. But how you goin' to know who was up on the Black Range that day? There was no tracks. Might find out who was outa town and all that. But how you goin' to prove they went that way?"

"I'll make it two thousand if you stay and find out the truth," said Sam. "I don't mind saying that I'm scared."

Flo Dockerty said, "Make it another thousand and we'll think about it."

"We?" Buchanan lifted his eyebrows. "Did you say we?"

"Look at it this way. I already found out something from those deputies. Working here I can learn a lot more."

"And get yourself killed, maybe."

"For a thousand I'll take the chance. I ain't exactly crazy about stayin' here in this town, but I don't aim to

42

leave here broke," she said. She grinned. "Sam don't love me here in Culebra. Least he could do is let me earn get-away money."

Sam said, "Will you think it over, Buchanan?"

"Maybe." The girl was bound to get into trouble. He had begun to like her, she was feisty and brave. "I'll stick around another day."

Sam said, "There's something wrong in town. The bank —if it goes broke the town is dead, you know that. Walt's worried, too. He won't admit it, but he's worried."

"Is he countin' on the marshal and his men to do anything?"

"He hired the deputies. Hagen was appointed by the selectmen."

"And just who are they?"

"Well, there was my father. Walt, Doc Fullerton and Jody Teller. They'll have to elect another one, now."

"I see." Buchanan reflected. "I'll talk to Jody. I'm no hand at doin' puzzles. But I'll see."

Sam said, "I'd appreciate it. I truly would." He looked at Flo Dockerty. "I'm sorry. I mean—well, this isn't San Francisco."

"Run along, little boy," she said. "I'm learnin' to like older men."

Sam looked distraught, fingered his collar, then nodded and left, his cheeks pink. Buchanan eyed Flo.

"You fly right at 'em, don't you?"

She shrugged. "A dude is a dude when he acts like one. Buchanan, we can make a dollar here."

"I already got a dollar."

"I can always use another one or two. Furthermore, like Sam says, here's a town goin' to hell in a hack. You can feel it. I can feel it."

He thought of Jody's considerable interests in Culebra and surroundings. He thought of the deputies and their attitude. He was peaceable, but he hated being pushed.

He asked, "How about the gamblin' in here, this place?"

"Honest until stakes are high."

"Coverly's a dealer?"

"One of the best I ever saw. I've seen a few."

"Would you believe the marshal?"

"No!"

"Slick as an eel. Also that smilin' little snake, Frey."

"That's quite a basketful."

"Don't try 'em."

"Oh, I dunno. It's getting interestin'."

She sighed. "I declare. I think I'm smart. But you do fool the boots off me."

Coverly and Addie were returning to the table. Coverly had lost some color. Addie looked blank but adoring as usual. They sat down.

Coverly said, "Shipment was short. Always somethin' around this place. You wouldn't want to buy it, would you, Buchanan?"

"With what?" Buchanan laughed. "I might stick around and see what happens, though. Never did own a saloon. Might be I'd get lucky."

"Poker game's open every night," said Coverly.

"I'll be droppin' in on it." Buchanan arose. "Seems like I might stick around awhile after all."

"You do that." But Coverly was listless. Some of the spark had gone from him. He took a deck of cards from his pocket and began to lay out a complicated solitaire.

Flo followed Buchanan to the door. "He's scared. Sam's scared. I'll keep my eyes and ears open."

"You do that."

"Older men. I never tried an older man." She showed a flash of her gold tooth.

"Don't try too hard." But he liked her grin, her flashing spirit. "See you later, little gal."

"Make sure you do, big man."

He walked down the street toward Jody's livery stable. There were people, ordinary people, going about their daily affairs. Everyone nodded in the friendly western fashion, a few called him by name. There were clerks from the mines, general store, bakery, saddlery. There were wives and plenty of children running here and there, playing, chasing dogs and cats. It was a growing town and in it dwelt many various people. If the town was threatened, the people would suffer because a town is people, he ruminated. It did not seem fair that a few selfish men should hurt a whole community full of people.

Chapter Four

Buchanan put down his belongings in the stable yard and looked again for Jody Teller. The hired hands, Mexican-Americans, grinned and shrugged. The boss did not confide in them, all they knew was that he had saddled one of his hacks and departed early in the morning. Nightshade nickered and he went into the barn to bestow an apple upon the black horse. When he came out Jody was riding into the yard.

One of the hostlers went to the head of the hack and Jody dismounted, wearily, somber. He looked at Buchanan's luggage and seemed to brighten just a trifle.

"So you're leavin' again? Just as well, maybe."

"Matter of fact," said Buchanan, "I'm stayin' around a spell. Gettin' out from underfoot, though. Thought I'd move to the hotel."

"Now, Buck, you know you can stay here as long as you want."

"Batchin' it for one is enough. Two—that's a mess."

"Well, here let me help with that stuff." He was not insistent, he seemed a bit listless, maybe worried.

They walked toward the hotel across the street and down at the middle of the town. The sign read "Culebra House" and it was two stories and deep. Buchanan had picked a room on the second floor facing the street.

He said, "Never knew you to take early rides, Jody. Nice day for it, though."

"Yeah, nice day."

"You oughta remember, old Sam Dade took an early ride."

"I ain't about to tote what he was carryin'."

"Fifty thousand dollars?" Buchanan asked quietly.

Jody answered, "You know about it. That why you're stickin' around?"

"Maybe." There was something odd about Jody, something that had not been there before.

They spoke no more, going into the hotel. The owner's name was Abuzzo, a dark man who brooded, father of many children with a fat wife in the kitchen, one of the few Italians in that part of the country. He scarcely looked up as Buchanan led the way to his room.

It was a large chamber, neat and clean, with the usual bed, bureau, wardrobe-closet, washstand. The window let out onto the roof of the veranda. The morning sun shone brightly on an Indian rug and a chamber pot well scrubbed and white against the bright colors of the rug.

Buchanan unslung his rifle and began to put away his dude clothing and spare shirts and underwear. Jody watched, disinterested, not chattering as was his habit.

"I got a feelin' you'd rather I pulled up my stake," Buchanan said. "Anything you wanta tell me?"

"You're goin' to get into this . . . business?"

Buchanan said, "I did find a dead man. Like I say, I know he was murdered. Tell me, Jody, how come you allowed 'em to hire Hempel and Frey?"

"They got their uses." Jody looked out of the window.

"Not when it comes to catchin' a killer." Buchanan paused, then added, "More like they'd be on the other side."

"Walt brought 'em in."

"Walt's an easterner. Now I wonder where he found a couple of gunslingers?"

"He found 'em. I thought maybe Hagen knew 'em, but I reckon he didn't."

"You reckon? You don't know?"

Jody said, "I don't know as much as I thought I did about anything. This town—I got everything I saved for years in this town. You can't blame a man for wantin' to hold on."

"Not blamin' anybody for anything," said Buchanan. "Just ponderin'."

"I know you when you ponder," said Jody. "Trouble comes and seeks you out when you ponder."

"Could be." He suddenly knew he shouldn't reveal to Jody any of the things that had been said and considered.

"Well, I'll be going. Hope everything turns out all right."

Jody's voice sounded hollow as he left the room.

Buchanan went about his orderly unpacking, bemused. Something was wrong with Jody, that was for sure. The whole town was in wrong, he thought. There was danger in the air, he knew well the odor of it. He put his rifle near the head of the bed and strapped on his six-gun with reluctance. It was not a time to go unarmed.

There was a tap on the door. He went to it, grasped the knob, threw it open as he drew the gun. Flo Dockerty squeaked and ran past him. The sunlight shown on her, making it clear that she was wearing a dressing robe with very little between it and her skin.

"Don't you point that thing at me!" she said. "I don't like guns."

"You and Coco," said Buchanan. "I'm plumb sorry. This town's got me skittery."

"Your friend," she said, settling herself in the only chair. "He's got the wind up, too."

"How do you know?"

Her gold tooth gleamed. She jumped up, took the tumbler from alongside the wash basin and ran to the wall. She placed the glass against the wall, her ear to the glass.

"Only this is kinda heavy. I keep one from the saloon around so I won't miss anything. Works fine. A Pinkerton I knew taught it to me."

"You're a sneaky one." But she amused him. "So, what about Jody Teller?"

"Scared like the others," she said. "You know it."

He nodded. "I got a whiff of it."

"They got a poker game set for tonight."

"Well, what of it?"

"They ain't spreadin' the word. Poker players always want customers, right?"

"Mostly."

"Hagen's not invited. Only Frey, Hempel, Dick and Walt Store. That's four."

"I see. They should be lookin' for five."

"I figure you'll oblige." She squinted at him, grinning. "You said they were slippery-fingered."

"You want me to be busted?"

She mocked his Texas drawl. "I'd sure admire to see 'em try it."

"You put a heap o' store in me, seems like. Happens I can't make it rain nor anything like that."

"I wouldn't bet on it." She was frankly admiring. "Remember what I told you? I know men."

"I remember."

"Furthermore," she said, "I got sharp eyes. I can see a fly walkin' on the moon."

"You could get in trouble seein' too much."

"Not if they don't catch me signalin' to you. If I see a cheat I'll touch my hair. See, like this, like I'm pushin' back a stray lock."

"Look, Flo. Just don't bother, huh?"

"Why not?"

"Somebody might notice. Just leave me to my own little ways, will you please?"

"But supposin' . . . ?"

"Supposin' nothin'. Keep your ears open. See what you can. But no signals."

"You're worried about me." This seemed to please her inordinately.

"Little old gal like you, wouldn't want to see you in trouble."

She skipped across the room and leaped to throw her arms around his neck. She planted a big kiss on him, dangling, kicking her heels. It was not unpleasant, but he plucked her loose and set her on her feet.

He said, "Not with the window wide open. Look yonder."

Across the street a half dozen urchins were leaping and giggling and staring. Marshal Hagen appeared, looked up, touched his hat and routed the young ones. Then he grinned broadly and went on his way.

"A gal can get a bad reputation that way," Buchanan said gravely.

For a moment she was disconcerted, then she snapped,

"A saloon gal's got no more reputation than an alley cat. So what?"

She ran out of the room. He went to the window. Culebra was going about its business. It was noon and the sun was high and harsh, throwing no shadows. All the color had gone out of the town.

When he arrived at the Silver Dollar it was early night. The place was almost deserted, as though a blight had fallen upon it all of a sudden. He went to the bar and ordered a beer. Flo came in her short-skirted costume and sat with him, calm and collected.

She said, "The deputies were talkin' to Dick Coverly. I couldn't hear what they were sayin', but he kept shakin' his head. Now he and Addie are upstairs and she's been cryin' a lot."

"I'll see if he'll talk to me." But before he could move from the bar the deputies came in with Walt Store. When they saw him they showed no concern. They went to a poker table and sat down. Coverly came from the rear with Addie close behind. Addie's eyes were swollen, her color was bad.

Walt Store called from the table, "Buchanan, we could use a fifth player here."

"Don't mind if I do." As he pulled away from the bar Flo gave him a quick amazed glance. This was not part of the plan as she had heard it.

Then Jody Teller came in. He stopped dead when he saw Buchanan headed for the poker table. He took a deep breath, then moved slowly but with determination toward the group. Coverly was already seated, breaking out new decks of cards.

Flo moved away from the bar, following Buchanan, veered and went to Addie. The two girls exchanged frightened stares. Another customer left the Silver Dollar and the place seemed to dim as though the oil lamps had been turned down, although no one had gone near the lamps. The barkeep positioned himself where he could watch the table and Buchanan knew there must be a shotgun down somewhere near his hand. He was a slick-haired man with a dragoon's mustache and he did not seem to be comfortable.

Store said, "Jody, you going to take a hand?"

"I'll just watch tonight." He took the lookout chair behind Buchanan, a high perch. He was wearing a gun beneath his coat, Buchanan saw. They were all wearing guns. Coverly's was under his arm, the gambler's holster, probably a short barreled .38. Store's weapon was a hideout derringer but Buchanan's trained eye detected it.

Altogether a setting loaded with dynamite, he thought. Once he had witnessed, unwillingly, a hanging. He had never forgotten the strained, solemn, nightmarelike atmosphere, the impending doom hovering over the assemblage, the victim, the Sheriff with his knotted rope. He felt it now.

There was one space vacant, between Hempel on his right and Coverly on his left. Buchanan took it. Store was beyond Coverly and Frey beside Store. Jody was silent, but then he had been uncharacteristically silent that morning.

In an attempt to lighten the mood, Buchanan asked, "Where's the professor?"

"His night off," said Coverly. "He don't play when we have the game."

"Why don't the girls take the evening off, then?" asked Store pleasantly.

"Up to them." Coverly was detached, unsmiling, a handsome young man with clever fingers, shuffling the deck.

"Well, what are we playing for?" asked Buchanan.

"Ten open, twenty raise," said Coverly. "No limit on raises."

Buchanan whistled. "Steep for me."

"Nobody sandbags in this bunch," said Store, his smile still easy if a trifle strained. "Just friendly poker."

Frey stifled a chuckle and Hempel dug at him with a sharp clbow.

A black bird was hovering, Buchanan thought. He could not be certain which shoulder it would land upon, that was the problem. He tilted his hat over his eyes and studied them as unobtrusively as possible. He caught a glimpse of Flo's face, a bit pinched, her eyes large as saucers. She had lost the skein, she knew no more than he did.

Addie felt it. She lived upstairs over the Silver Dollar, ever near to Coverly. She danced with the customers, she sat with them while they drank, but that was as far as she ever went, Flo had reported. Now her roving eyes showed constant attention, trepidation, as she concentrated on Coverly's every move.

Coverly shoveled out the cards. Buchanan wondered why young Sam Dade was not among those present. It seemed wrong, but maybe it was by careful design. He watched the first ace drop in front of him and took the deck to deal.

He anted up ten dollars. He shuffled. His big hands made him appear clumsy. The players regarded him with amusement.

"Need a basket, there?" Frey asked.

"Seems like it," Buchanan was apologetic. "Uh—draw poker, right?"

"Anything opens," said Coverly.

"Can I buy four cards?" demanded Frey.

"Pay your money and you can buy five," said Coverly, his voice brittle.

Under cover of his seeming clumsiness, Buchanan was examining the cards for markings. He found none. He dealt slowly, honestly; first to Coverly, then Store, Frey, Hempel, himself. They picked up their hands but he had a strong feeling that the value of the hands was only a lead-in to more important business.

He edged his cards. He had dealt himself, he found, three aces. Like all card players he could be lucky in streaks. This might well be one of those times. He caught Flo edging closer, reading the hands of the others with sharp eyes. He gave her a hard glare.

Coverly said, "Open for ten."

They all played, expressionless until it came to the dealer. Buchanan debated with himself. He must raise. He might learn something by their reaction. Finally he said, "Raise—uh—twenty dollars."

Behind him on the high stool Jody shifted so that the

seat creaked. Buchanan could feel the man's eyes boring into his back.

Coverly said, "I'll play along."

Store and Frey also played. Hempel laughed in his surly manner and put in forty dollars, crowing, "Ha! Right into me."

Buchanan said, "How about that?" He matched the twenty-dollar raise. Then he said, "I just got to raise another twenty, seems like."

Coverly and Store shook their heads and folded their cards. Frey cursed under his breath, hesitated, then said, "I ain't throwin' good money after bad," as he flung down his hand.

Hempel snorted. There was a brief alteration of mood. Two gamblers head and head instilled some real excitement into the game. "Gimme a call—and gimme two tickets."

Buchanan dealt him the pair of cards. Then he took two for himself, pretending disgruntlement, as though he believed Hempel had been holding three of a kind higher than his own. Poker, he knew, consisted of theatrics directed against a suspected weakness of opponents.

Hempel said, "Now I betcha twenty!"

"Ten bet, twenty raise," Coverly said colorlessly.

"Ten then. I betcha ten." Hempel was not a man of subtlety.

Buchanan pretended to study his cards. He ground them in his big hands. He said, "Well, you did want to bet twenty. So I'll raise twenty. Give you a chance."

"And twenty more!" Hempel was beaming.

"Got to keep goin'," said Buchanan. "You makes your bed, you lay in it."

"Twenty more!"

"And twenty."

Hempel stopped grinning. He had still a couple of hundred dollars before him, more money than a deputy should own, Buchanan thought. But he was uneasy. He fiddled with his money, his cards, a brooding giant.

Then he said, "Hell, this is gettin' like sandbaggin'. Seein's you're new here, I'll call. Beat three kings."

Buchanan said, "Will three aces do it?" He spread out

53

the cards. He had bought a pair of fours to fill the hand. "Reckon a man has to bet them cards. Right?"

He took in the pot, fingers steady, carefully sorting and arranging gold and bills. Store was laughing at the glowering Hempel, who remained silent. Frey was thoughtful. Coverly had lost interest again. Jody moved again on the squeaky chair. Flo was smiling, showing her tooth with its gold cap. Addie had not changed expression, her color had not returned.

Coverly took the deck and Buchanan watched his darting, clever white hands. The man was a dealer, all right. He had all the moves. He was also dealing with strict honesty. The man did not live who could deceive Buchanan dealing cards.

He held a bust this time. He watched Store open, Frey and Hempel play. Coverly also bought cards. There was nothing exciting in this hand as Store won with a pair of kings. Buchanan won the next hand with a small straight. Hempel then dealt him a four flush under the guns and he opened, pushing his luck. Everyone played for ten dollars.

He peeked at his draw. It was another spade, so that he held an ace-high flush. He pushed out ten dollars.

Coverly called on a three-card buy. Store called, and Frey dropped. Hempel had also taken one card. He raised twenty.

Buchanan said, "Seems like you and me all the time. I just got twenty more says it's mine."

"And another twenty."

Buchanan debated. If Hempel had two pairs before the draw, sitting where he was, he should have raised, shutting out the peddlers. Good before the draw, nothing after the draw, that was two pairs. But raising, he might have filled two pairs after neglecting to raise. He looked at his own cards, not sure of the play now.

It was best to call. He did so, saying "Flush to the ace."

Hempel flung his hand face up in the middle of the table.

"Damn it! King high in hearts." He had also filled a flush.

"Some days you can't make a nickel," said Buchanan, raking in the pot.

He dealt. Again he held threes, this time tens. He was

54

on a lucky run, no doubt about it. He raised Coverly's openers and won the hand.

Coverly said, "How about a hand of stud for a change?"

"Anything to bust this guy's luck," said Hempel. Yet the big deputy was not really angered, Buchanan thought. There was still something more in the air.

Coverly dealt them, one face down, one face up. Store showed an ace, Frey a ten, Hempel a king, Buchanan a queen. Coverly dealt himself a three of hearts.

Store bet. Everyone stayed, Coverly hesitating, eyeing his hole card, then putting in his ten dollars. He had not yet won a pot. He dealt them around, a four to Store, a deuce to Frey, another king to Hempel. Then he gave Buchanan a seven and himself another three.

Hempel said, "Bets ten."

No one raised against the pair of kings. Coverly ran the cards, his hands swift as the wings of hummingbirds. Store got an eight, Frey a six, Hempel another six, Buchanan a seven to make a pair. Coverly drew a four spot.

Hempel bet. Buchanan hesitated, then went along only because he was a winner. Coverly again paused, but put in his ten. Store and Frey stayed, so they must each have a hole card that matched, Buchanan thought.

Coverly dealt. No one paired. The air was deadly still in the saloon although it was not a big hand. Buchanan watched every move around the table. Coverly was about to deal himself his last card.

It all happened at once. Marshal Hagen came through the door on his nightly rounds. Hempel let out a roar and lunged across in front of Buchanan yelling, "I saw that!"

His big hand struck Coverly's wrist. The three of spades fell to the table top.

Jody came down off the high stool and got between Buchanan and Coverly. Addie ran and screamed.

Buchanan threw Hempel from him. The big man was heavy. He bounced from the table even as he drew his gun. He fired going down to the floor.

Coverly had his gun out. He got off one shot. It went into the ceiling. Hempel's bullet struck Coverly in the head and the handsome features went red, then white.

Hagen's voice filled the room. "Don't anybody move."

The marshal was holding his Colt on the assembly. Addie, moaning, threw herself on the body of Coverly. The gambler was already dead.

Buchanan disengaged himself from Jody Teller. Flo was against the bar. The barkeep had the shotgun on the surface of the bar but was raising his hands as Hagen dominated the scene.

Hempel got to his feet and glared at Buchanan. "You seen it. Everybody seen it. That jackleg tinhorn's been cheatin' us right along."

Frey said, "I seen him get it outa his sleeve, all right."

Hagen looked at Walt Store, the banker. "What about it?"

Store sighed and shook his head. His cheeks were white. "I'm afraid that's right, Marshal. I saw it."

Hagen swung around, staring, "Buchanan?"

There was a brief silence. Then Buchanan said, "No."

"No—what?"

He went to the dead man and gently picked up Addie, looking for Flo, who came running. Addie was sobbing her heart out. Flo dragged her away by main force. Buchanan turned back the dead man's sleeves.

He said, "No holdout."

"He was gettin' 'it' outa there somehow," roared Hempel. "I seen the edge of the card."

"He was sharp," chimed in Frey.

"Yes, I must confess I saw the flicker of the card," said Walt Store. "I'm sorry. I mean—a man shouldn't be killed for it, should he, now?"

"Them's the rules," Hempel said harshly. "You get caught, you be ready with your own gun. He knew it."

"He did draw his weapon," Store said. "I don't like this. Run a man out of town, yes. But to kill him? I don't like it at all."

Buchanan arose and surveyed the saloon. The two customers had hastily departed. There was nothing to be said, too many witnesses had testified that Coverly was in the act of cheating, drawing a lousy three spot, at that. Hagen was sending the bartender for Dr. Dudley. There was no question of the verdict of Culebra. Hempel would be justified. He lifted a shoulder and turned away.

Jody Teller said in his ear, "Stay out of it."

"You kept me out of it. You and Hagen," said Buchanan bleakly.

"It's for the best," Jody urged. "This whole town is in a mess."

Addie broke free of the smaller Flo and came rushing. "You murdered him! Liars! Bunch of crooks! I'll get even with you! One way or the other, I'll getcha for this!"

Hagen holstered his gun and went to her. When he touched her elbow, solicitous, yearning, she shoved him so that he almost fell.

"Lawman! Banker! All of you! You murdered him. You'll pay. You'll suffer."

Buchanan put his arms around her. He held her and walked her away. Flo showed him the stairs. He carried the girl to the second floor. There was nothing to be gained standing around with post mortems over a dead man. He took her into the room indicated by Flo and closed the door and turned a key in the lock.

He said, "Flo, listen and make sure nobody gets close."

She said, "Buchanan."

"Yes?"

"Dick didn't slick that trey."

"Who did?"

"It had to be Hempel when he went over at him. I told you Hempel is slicker than he looks. It had to be him."

Addie shivered, but was suddenly calmer. "You know that, Flo? I mean, you know Dick didn't do it?"

"She knows it," Buchanan told her. "And I know it."

Addie dashed tears from her eyes. "You both know it?"

"It don't make sense," Buchanan said. "If Flo knows Hempel and Frey are card sharpers, then Dick knew it. He wouldn't try a thing like that in a small pot. Just don't figure out. It was a frame. But it appeared to me like Dick sort of knew somethin' was comin'."

Addie gulped but went on, "He knew somethin' he

wouldn't tell me. I tried and tried but he just sat and stared at the walls. He owes—owed—the bank a lot of money for the fixin's of the bar and all."

"The bank," said Buchanan. "Yeah, the bank, it all comes back to the bank."

"Dick wasn't bad," Addie said. "He wanted the best of everything for me and for him. Where was that damn Hagen while Dick was gettin' killed? Tell me that."

"Doin' his job. I don't blame him," said Buchanan. "I got to take some blame my own self. I should've been able to stop it. They outsmarted me."

Flo said from her place at the door, "You and me."

"They asked me into the game because if I was watchin' I might have a chance to butt in." Buchanan reconstructed it in his mind. "They edged me in where they could get at Dick and interfere with me. Jody Teller, my old friend."

"You think he was in on it?"

"I don't know. This whole town is into somethin' and it goes back before Dan Dade was robbed and killed, that's for sure."

"Addie stared at him. "Mr. Store, is he part of it?"

"Who invited me into the game?"

She thought a moment. "But Mr. Store was Dick's friend. He lent him the money."

"And took a mortgage. The Silver Dollar's a valuable property," said Buchanan. "In this town I trust two people. You and Flo."

"That's crazy," said Addie. "We're just saloon girls."

"I wouldn't put it that way," he told her.

"Me neither," Flo said. "Only there's another trouble. We're out of work."

"There's no other place in town to work," said Addie. Her freckles stood out, watered by tears. "If I could help, do somethin', I'd feel better, I tell you that."

He looked at her. She should have stayed on the farm, the ranch, wherever she came from, he thought. She did not belong in a saloon. Flo was different, Flo could take care of herself, he felt. Addie was vulnerable.

He asked, "Look, could you be nice to Tim Hagen?"

"No!"

"Just let him console you, treat you good?"

"No!"

"If it would help?"

She said, "I don't see how it would help."

"Thing is, we don't truly know about Hagen. Looks to me like the deputies have got him sorta blocked in. Looks like the selectmen hired them and Hagen's got to live with it or quit. Supposin' the reason he don't quit is because he's gone on you, Addie?"

"I still don't see how it would do any good to play up to him. He's nobody. Nothin'."

"He's the law," Buchanan said. "He wears the badge. I'd like to know more about him."

"But we won't be here. I haven't any money to live on without workin'." Addie was confused.

"I've got a notion about that," said Buchanan.

At the door, Flo said, "Someone's comin' down the hall."

"I'll lay odds it's Hagen." He fixed Addie with his eyes. "Do the best you can and I'll find out for you. It's not who killed Dick, we know that. It's why."

"You'll take care of them?" Her voice was low and hard.

"That's a promise."

"I don't know." Tears ran down her cheeks. "I don't know what to do or say."

Flo opened the door. The marshal stood, hesitant, removing the hat from his smooth, blond head. "Is she all right? Could I see her?"

Buchanan said, "She'll tell you the truth. Coverly was not holding out a three spot."

"But they all testified he did. Said they saw it."

"You goin' to do anything about it?"

"I'm hogtied. My own deputies, Mr. Store, there's no way I can hang it on Hempel."

"Do you owe the bank any money?"

"Why, no." Hagen seemed surprised.

"But there's some strings on you."

He flushed. "You got no call to say that."

"All right, then look for reasons why Coverly was framed. Addie, you said he was upset. Since when?"

"Since the liquor was delivered, remember? While the

59

cases were bein' brought in Hempel and Frey talked to Dick. I tried to hear what was said. I don't know—it's been worrisome."

"What's been worrisome?"

"Oh, things." She was lost again. "I only know that afterwards Dick wasn't right. Wasn't himself, like."

Buchanan said, "Flo, let's you and me take a walk."

The Silver Dollar bar was now full of animated people talking loudly about the killing of Dick Coverly. The barkeep was sweating, running up and down, falling behind in the orders. Buchanan steered Flo out the back way, through the storehouse to the alley. On Main Street they turned toward the bank, Flo trotting, taking two steps to Buchanan's one, long stride.

He said, "I should've prevented it. I smelled it comin'. I just didn't know who was goin' to get it."

"You keep saying that. But we were both watching and neither of us caught on. And then they kept you out of it."

"Coverly was in on somethin'," he ruminated. "They were after him to take some step or other. He wouldn't do it. They set him up. Funny thing, he just took it. Like he knew there was no way out."

"Because the whole town's in on it?"

"That's the way it looks."

There was a light in the rear of the bank. Buchanan led Flo to a window through which Sam Dade could be seen at a desk, poring over a huge ledger. He started when he heard a tap on the window, peered out. Then he came through the bank, unlocked the back door and beckoned them in.

"Hereafter I'd put a shade on that window," said Buchanan. "I also wouldn't work in there at night and alone."

"I heard what happened," said Sam. He ran a hand through his hair. He was agitated. "Walt told me."

"Your partner's a damn liar," said Buchanan.

"I've been wondering lately."

"He said he saw Coverly get a card from his sleeve. It didn't happen that way."

"I believe you. I've been going over the books again and again. Something's damn wrong. Money disappears, then turns up. Different people make deposits. I wish I'd paid more attention to business. I'm lost among a bunch of figures. But I'll keep trying."

"About the Silver Dollar," said Buchanan.

"The mortgage? Yes, we'll have to take over."

"You need a manager."

"Yes, we'll have to find one."

"You're lookin' at him," said Buchanan.

"You?"

"Nobody else. Flo, here, she'll help, she knows the business. And we'll keep Addie on."

"What are you getting at?"

"The truth," said Buchanan. "A man got killed. I should've stopped it. My old friend Jody Teller helped keep me from it. One way or another I got to do somethin'. Managin' the saloon will give me an excuse to stick around. Only Jody knows the real reason outside of you and Flo and now Addie. I want to see what happens."

"Suppose Walt hollers about it?"

"Sam, you got to take a stand. You got to assert yourself. Store won't yell too loud. He can't open up too much. As it is, too many people are in this thing to make it foolproof. Whoever is bossin' the deal is smart enough to lay low and play it out little by little."

"You think it's Walt?"

"I don't know. I don't see the real reasonin' behind it all. That's what I want to find out."

Sam walked up and down. Then he said, "You've got the job."

"I'll be takin' over right now. Business is jumpin' over there."

"Can I say you offered to take it on a percentage of the take? That we're getting you cheap?"

"You tell Walt that. Later he'll find out the cost."

He took Flo out of the bank before Sam could change his mind. The walk back to the saloon was at a slower pace. Buchanan was silent, thinking.

Flo said, "You shouldn't blame yourself."

"I got to."

"You need action." She was shrewd, divining. "This is a confusion. You need to clear out the cobwebs."

"Cobwebs is right. There's spiders around and one of 'em is very good at spinnin' webs."

They came to the Silver Dollar. The noise in the bar had increased. They stood in the doorway. The two customers who had been in the bar when the shootout began were arguing. They each had seen it a different way. Half-drunken customers were lined up on each side. Fists were brandished. The barkeep was trying to shut them up.

Buchanan removed his gun belt. He handed it to Flo and said, "Looks like we might have that action. I'm a peaceable man, but things can get outa hand."

Flo staggered under the weight of the armament but chuckled and said, "Take over, Buchanan."

He pushed into the crowd, now beginning to mill. He picked up two small men, one in each hand, and set them aside. His voice rose above the sound.

"Just hold it, everybody."

They wheeled upon him and stared. He towered above them, grinning a bit.

"I'm takin' over the management of this joint," he told them. "Now simmer down, please."

One of the men who had witnessed the beginning of the shootout yelled, "He's one of 'em. He set there and let Rick be killed! Now he owns the joint!"

Someone shouted, "Let's get 'im!"

Buchanan waved one loglike arm. Three men went reeling across the room. Another picked up a bottle. Buchanan dropped a negligent fist against his head. The man did a somersault in the sawdust.

The bartender gasped, "I got 'em!" He had the shotgun in his hands, sweat glistening on his face. "Lemme have them, Buchanan."

"Just hold it steady." Buchanan grabbed another combatant. He leveled the man off in his arms, then threw him into the crowd. A half-dozen went down kicking.

Marshal Hagen came down the stairs, gun drawn. Buchanan waved him off and met the charge of two burly miners.

He hit one in the belly. He cuffed the other behind the ear. Both went down.

Now there was a clearing, a circle around Buchanan. He put his back against the bar and said, "That's enough exercise for tonight. Drinks are on the house."

The men in the back pushed the men in the front but the man in the foreground did not want to get within his reach. Hagen walked among them. They fell back, then stepped over the only two men Buchanan had struck with his fist and someone laughed.

"I'll take the drink," said one of those who had been manhandled. "By God, I need it."

"One question," Buchanan said. "Where were you all tonight when the shootin' began?"

A voice called, "We was warned to stay away."

"Who warned you?"

"Why, I dunno." The man took off his hat and scratched his head. "It's just the word went around, like."

There was no use to ask further. Buchanan put a hand on the bar and vaulted it. This was a new experience, never in his adventurous career had he tended bar. He did the best he could as the customers picked up the two dazed men he had punched and propped them up for their free libation.

He asked the bartender, "What's your name?"

"Brannigan," said the man. He was bone weary. "This has been one hell of a night. You really takin' over?"

"Yes. I'm going to hire another man tomorrow. And Brannigan, keep your ears and eyes wide open."

"For what?"

"Anything I might want to know. Okay?"

"Sure, Buchanan. Sure."

He sensed that Brannigan was suffering from the Culebra disease—he was afraid of something. "Did Dick hire you?"

"Well . . . sure."

"Who recommended you to Dick?"

"Mr. Store did. He knowed me from before."

"I see." But he only saw it dimly, he thought. He needed proof and there was none.

Flo was at the piano, playing and singing for the crowd. He had not known she could play—he made a mental

63

note to fire the professor and save a salary. The customers were spending like drunken sailors or cowboys on a pay night. Poor Coverly, he thought, a night's business like this would have helped pay on the mortgage.

Chapter Five

Early in the morning Buchanan rode Nightshade into the country south of Culebra. Here were the farms, the ranches lush with grama grass where produce was grown and cattle could thrive. One piece of land seemed unattended and he rode off and up a trail.

There was a farmhouse, empty. Signs of dilapidation were already setting in. Yet the land seemed as rich as any surrounding it. A wild dog howled and then ran off, tail between its legs.

Buchanan remounted and rode across the fields, fixing landmarks in his mind, should he come this way again. He rode a foothill where loose shale rattled beneath the hooves of Nightshade.

He saw cattle. He rode toward them, but the cows were not branded; they tossed their horns and skittered away. He rode on and found a line cabin, also deserted. He went inside the low-ceiling building. There was a stove and he examined it. The ashes were not warm, but he knew there had been a fire recently. He searched the place and found cigar butts, scraps of food.

He rode again, looking for the ranch house. When he found it there were the same signs of vacancy and ruin as he had seen at the farmhouse. It seemed strange, a deserted ranch on which the line cabin had been used within the week. A meeting place? he wondered. But for whom and why a meeting out here beyond town? He remembered Jody's early ride.

He decided to return to town and ask some questions. He rode back to the main trail. He was going over a knoll when a bullet whistled its little tune close to his ear. He bent low and spurred Nightshade and the big, swift horse took off like the wind. Another shot followed but shattered only a low hanging branch. He was, Buchanan imagined, out of range for good marksmanship.

He had been observed, he knew. Had he been followed? If so, by whom?

Too many questions with no answers, he thought. He put Nightshade in Jody's stable and walked slowly to the bank. Walt Store was busy with a customer. Buchanan went into Sam Dade's office.

"Been ridin'," he said. He described the empty farmhouse, the line cabin. "How come?"

"Foreclosures." Sam's brow was furrowed. "Damn rotten business. Two families, the Cortrights and the Daleys. They had a little hard luck and the old man and Walt closed 'em out."

"How come no tenants? Pretty dumb to let good land lay there earnin' nothin'."

"I don't understand it, either. Walt said he'd tried but couldn't get anybody to take them over. But I can't find any advertisements for them." He picked up a newspaper. "I did find this, thought you might want to see it."

There was a story datelined Sacramento. The headline read *Prizefight Broken Up*. It seemed that one Coco Bean and one Joe Konecke were matched in an oak grove outside town and the Sheriff had raided the scene, arresting both men. The judge had given them ten days in the local jail to think it over.

"Poor Coco. He purely despises jails," said Buchanan. "He'll be out of my hair for awhile at least."

Sam said, "Too bad. He probably lost his purse, too."

"He'll be all right. I'm thinkin' about this trouble in Culebra."

"I'm working on the books. I'm counting every two-bit piece in the safe. If there was a run on us, we'd be busted. The town would be bankrupt. There's been some crooked work, I know that, but I'm not bookkeeper enough to ferret it out. I'm sending for auditors. Maybe we can get to the bottom of it that way."

"Good idea," said Buchanan.

He went down to the saloon. Flo was in the office going over Coverly's books. She pointed her sharp little face at

Buchanan and said, "Coverly wasn't great at keepin' accounts but one thing's plain. This joint always took in plenty."

"Then why was the mortgage so big?"

"Couldn't answer that. Lots of cash paid entries. For what?"

Buchanan said, "Everything runs back to the bank. But why should a bank try to ruin a prosperous town?"

"Maybe Sam will find out. Maybe the auditors will learn somethin'."

"Maybe Jody knows something. Maybe the moon's made of green cheese. So . . . we bury Rick Coverly."

She wrinkled her nose. "He wasn't a man you got to know right off. I wonder about him."

"How's Addie?"

"Better. Can't get any sense out of her, though. I better go and help her get ready for the buryin'."

"You do that." He went to the hotel and changed into his San Francisco garb. His mind worked over everything he had been able to learn or guess. Walt Store was the only man in town with the brains to set up such a rangdoodle. Jody didn't have it in him. Sam seemed honest, it had to be reckoned that he was honest. Furthermore, his father had been murdered, Buchanan was positive.

Fifty-thousand dollars or more had to be somewhere around. It was not in the bank. It was hidden and there had to be a reason for it. Sam had said the bank was almost broke. What would the auditors find?

And if Daniel Dade was toting all that money, where was he going with it? He had been riding over the Black Range, which led to no adjacent town. Was it a rendezvous? With whom?

Buchanan's head began to ache. He walked to the livery stable. Jody Teller was waiting with a buggy. The town was turning out for the funeral.

Jody said, "I sent a carriage for the gals and Brannigan."

"That's right nice of you." It was not the time to ask why Jody had interfered with him and allowed Coverly to be killed. His friend looked pale and weary and he was not by any means his usual loquacious self.

A hearse driven by a top-hatted undertaker came by.

The girls followed in Jody's carriage with Brannigan driving. Jody pulled into line. People rode and walked out to the neat, flat piece of ground that was the cemetery. The preacher was already there, black clad and solemn.

Conspicuously absent at the graveside were Store, Hempel, and Frey. Present were Sam Dade and Hagen. The throng formed a silent circle and the preacher said a few simple words. Buchanan, Jody, the marshal and Brannigan carried the pine box to the gaping hole and a few more words were spoken.

Addie, heavily veiled, stood straight, Flo at her side. She was composed. People stared, women whispered. Buchanan took off his hat. So far as he could see, none wept for the handsome young gambler who had so untimely been removed from the world. They came to watch and gossip, not to mourn.

But when the first spadeful of dirt was thrown upon the coffin Addie could not be budged. Flo tugged gently, then with more insistence but Addie lifted the veil and stood firm. The sunlight struck the freckles across her nose, the bright unshed tears, the straight line of her lips. People stared, then turned away with varying emotions. The preacher spoke to her, his face tight with the effort. She did not respond.

Buchanan said to Jody, "You go on with Brannigan. They'll be wanting a wake of sorts, I reckon."

Jody was looking at Addie. "A shame. She's a good sorta gal. A shame."

"Yes. A dirty shame." Buchanan stared at his friend. "And I'll be wanting to know how dirty it was."

Jody did not meet his gaze, beckoning to Brannigan, going to the buggy. Buchanan wondered how long before the man would crack. Jody had always been decent, before he acquired property and wealth.

"Blessed be nothin'," he murmured to himself, going to the two girls beside the grave.

The clods of dirt fell heavily on the wooden coffin, Buchanan stared down the lingering curious until the three of them were alone with the gravediggers.

Addie said, "When I was little I went to church and all.

I don't want to say bad things now. But I loved Dick. I truly loved him. He didn't do what they said. He was good to me, he was making a good business. He said we would be married."

"Sure, baby," Flo said. "We know."

"No. You don't know. Dick wasn't as smart as he looked. He was like me a lot. He would've married me. Then we were goin' to sell out, move away."

"It's too bad, I know," Flo said. "It's the toughest kinda luck."

"You don't believe it. But that's all right." She stared at Buchanan. "You'll get Hempel, won't you? And whoever put him up to it?"

"I'll get them," said Buchanan, meaning it, feeling for the girl, for the dead young man.

Addie bent and picked up a handful of dirt and crumbled it between her fingers and dropped it into the grave. "Dust to dust. I remember that from my mama's funeral. That was when papa ran away and left us. . . ." She shook herself, making an effort. "I'll go now. Thanks, you people."

They walked toward the carriage. Marshal Hagen stepped from behind the vehicle where he had been waiting. His hat was in his hands. He wore a black kerchief around his neck and his mien was deprecatory.

"Didn't want to butt in, folks. If I could do anything?"

Buchanan pressed Addie's arm and she climbed into the rear seat of the rig. "Ride in with us, Marshal."

Hagen climbed in beside Addie, not touching her, his hat still in his grasp. "You know I'm sorry. I mean, no man should go like that, him so young and all."

She said, "Thank you, Tim."

Buchanan clucked to the horses. They drove back to the Silver Dollar. Addie descended on Hagen's arm, ran into the saloon. Flo went after her. Hagen stood staring after them. Buchanan spoke softly.

"You got to give her time. Lots of time."

Hagen put on his hat, his attitude uncertain, between longing and despair. "Maybe I haven't got time. Maybe I won't last in this job of marshal."

"Why not?"

"Too many things are happenin' that I can't handle."

"You're the law. It's your job to try and handle things, lots of things."

Hagen looked hard at him. "You think I'm scared, don't you?"

"If you ain't, you're a damn fool. And remember, the measure of a man is how he acts when he's scared." Buchanan drove the carriage back to the livery stable. Hagen stood and watched him go, his eyes haunted, his face shadowed.

When Buchanan arrived Jody's buggy was not in sight. The opportunity to talk with him was lost. The hostlers obviously knew nothing. He left the carriage and walked back to the Silver Dollar. He was gloomy and restive. He was not much for towns in any case, and Culebra was getting him down. He struggled to regain his normally optimistic balance regarding life.

The saloon was roaring with customers. Men who had scarcely known Coverly drank to his salvation. Death had made all men boon companions that afternoon. Buchanan went into the office and found Flo seated, deep in thought. "Addie okay?" he asked.

"She's got a bottle of booze. And she's not much of a drinker."

"That's bad."

"Maybe. Maybe she needs it."

"You know men. I know women. It's bad," he told her. "They framed Dick. Hempel, Frey, and Store. Seein's Store lied, he's in it."

"We got to do something. But what?" she asked.

"Hang around. Listen. Ask questions. Think. Use the sense God gave us."

"It's a big order," she said, showing her tooth again. "But I'll go out there and try it."

She went into the saloon. Buchanan sat behind Coverly's desk. There had been nothing but the incomplete ledger, no correspondence, no scraps of paper, nothing. It did nothing to breach the wall. Someone must have made sure of that.

Restless, he went into the bar. Flo was talking with a

lean stranger in range clothing, a medium-tall man still dusty from road travel. Buchanan drifted over to them.

Flo said, "Mr. Buchanan, this here is Lone Tom Jones. Lookin' for work, he says."

"Well, fine." The man was about thirty and had a pleasant look about him. His eyes were sharp and intelligent. He stood hipshot like a rider accustomed to high-heeled boots. Buchanan had seen a thousand like him. "Have one on the house, Jones."

"That's neighborly of you." He drained the glass before him and accepted another. "Hear you had a shootin'."

"Buried him this afternoon."

"Well, everybody's gotta go sometime." Jones sipped his whiskey. "You don't happen to know of a job around, do you?"

"No, but it's a busy town. You'll find somethin'." Buchanan moved on, restless.

Flo went to the piano and played and sang. She chose hymns and after a moment some of the men joined in, their voices low out of respect for the dead. Later, when the liquor was in, they would be whooping it up, Buchanan knew, it was the way of men.

Hagen came in. He came to Buchanan and asked the inevitable question about Addie, as though days had passed.

"Maybe you better go up and have a word with her," Buchanan suggested. "Flo says she's not too pert."

"I might do just that." Hagen turned away. Then he stopped, looked at Jones standing near the end of the bar. "Say, who's that stranger?"

"Name of Lone Tom Jones, he tells it."

Hagen reached inside his vest and took out a folded piece of paper. "One thing I got is a memory for faces. Take a look at this."

It was a wanted dodger and there were two views of the man's face, full and side. Buchanan glanced from it to "Jones." He read, *Sandy Folger, wanted for robbery.* "You have got a good memory, Hagen."

"Will you watch the crowd? The boys are drinkin', they might get feisty."

"Right," said Buchanan. He moved to where he had a commanding position. "Go to it."

Hagen walked quietly behind the wanted man. He said, "Sandy, you're under arrest."

The man raised his hands. Then he turned around and faced Hagen. "I'm peaceable. I don't want no trouble."

Hagen said, "The belt. Drop it and be careful."

Someone yelled, "Is that damn marshal spoilin' the fun?"

"No fun," Buchanan said sharply. "Everybody stay still."

The rider dropped the gun belt. Hagen picked it up, never relaxing his vigilance. "The jail's right on down the street."

"How about my hoss?"

"It'll be taken care of. Walk slow and easy now, Sandy."

"Yes, sir." He shrugged and went ahead of the marshal, out through the doors of the saloon.

"What was that?" Flo asked.

"Hagen caught himself a wanted man," said Buchanan. "Did it just right, too. No fuss, no muss."

"You mean Lone Tom is a criminal?"

"That's what the dodger said. By the time they find out who wants him and for what, we'll know more about it."

"All we need's another crook in town," said Flo. She went back to the piano.

Buchanan went upstairs. The door to Addie's room was ajar. He looked in and she was asleep. He saw a half-empty bottle of whiskey beside the bed. He went in and took it, pausing to look around. He had not been in this room before. It was large but undistinguished, a window on the alley, two closets, a few knicknacks on a dresser, the bed, the bureau, almost as bare as Buchanan's hotel room.

He pulled a light quilt over the sleeping girl and stood looking down at her, sorrowing. She should have stayed wherever she was, any place was better than this for her. The west, it was always said, was fine for men, good for horses and rotten for dogs and women. Addie was a victim.

He caught a glimpse of himself in a mirror, a big man,

not inclined to brood, now thinking of his own boyhood in East Texas. His father had been a sheriff, his mother a handsome large lady dead in her thirties. "Sandlappers," they called people from that region so close to the softness of the Louisiana bayous, but they had been hardened by toil and love of the outdoors. They were a certain breed and he was proud of his Scottish inheritance.

The girl on the bed had no such early experience. She was not ready for the frontier life in towns. Flo Dockerty, now, she could handle it. She was another sort of woman.

In the mirror he suddenly realized that the man he saw was wearing the San Francisco clothing. It made him uncomfortable. He went out, closing the door softly behind him, returning to the saloon downstairs.

Hagen met him at the foot of the stairs. "He's our man, all right. He admits it, cool as a cucumber. I sent out some wires, Colorado, Texas, California, Wyoming."

"Busy fella, ain't he?" Buchanan was looking at the bar customers.

"He gets around. A bad hombre. How about Addie?" The marshal had a one-track mind.

"Better let her sleep. I just spotted another small problem. You might check it out." He went down the length of the long bar, Hagen trailing him.

The party was growing. Someone was lachrymose, intoning, " 'In the midst of life we are in death.' Poor ole Dick."

Three men drinking together caught sight of Buchanan's reflection in the bar mirror and turned to face him. Buchanan motioned Hagen in closer.

"Mr. Cook, the Krag brothers," he said. "From Frisco. Very tough cookies, they think."

Cook said, "It's a free country. You got no cause to be onto us."

"How come you're not in jail with Coco and Joe?"

"We ain't dumb, is why." Cook tugged at his bulbous nose. "Everybody don't do us in proper like you done."

"Everybody should. Reckon you know I'm running this place?"

"We heard."

"All the way to Frisco? People do talk a lot, don't they?" Buchanan squinted at them. "Maybe you came looking for me?"

"Not on your tintype. We're just lookin' for matches. Business. Jasper'll box anybody, any time."

"Culebra's not the place, not at this time. By the way, I want you to meet Marshal Hagen. You heard of law? He's the law." He looked at Spike. "He still carry that handy blackjack?"

Spike slid his cap to the other side of his head and said defiantly, "If I does, ye'll know it. Ain't no law."

"True, true." Buchanan winked at Hagen. "People carry guns an' everything around here."

"I ain't scared of no guns." Spike showed blackened teeth in what might have been a grin. "Me an' Jasper, we can handle ourselves."

"Now, we're right glad to hear that, right Marshal?"

"Right. A couple people haven't been able to," said Hagen. He looked worried again. "Too many people."

"I'm sure these boys'll be all right. Enjoy your drinks."

He went behind the bar. Brannigan handed him a sack of money. Buchanan took it into the back office to count it. Flo came in and sat down, cracking her knuckles.

"They never quit. Talk about an Irish wake."

He said, "Here, help me with this."

She began to count the bills and coins. It occurred to Buchanan that he was unarmed. He looked in a desk drawer and found a .38 caliber Smith & Wesson. He left the drawer open and went back to his task. Flo batted an eye, but did not interrupt.

When the money was totaled, Flo said, " I wish I owned this joint."

"The bank will do good."

"The bank, the bank. Walt Store." She shook her head "Make or break, which is it?"

"The bank was doing good business all along. Sam's trying to find out where the money went. The auditors will be here in a few days and then maybe we'll learn something."

"Hagen. What do you really make of him?"

Buchanan said, "I figure it remains to be seen."

74

"Whatever that means."

"It means there's got to be a showdown sooner or later. Maybe when the auditors get here. Then we'll know about the marshal."

"You mean he might be on the fence, sorta?"

"Or caught between the devil and the deep blue sea."

"Addie. If she could play along with him. Because, believe me . . ."

"You know men," interrupted Buchanan.

"Well, it's true."

"When Addie sobers up she'll feel Old Man Remorse. You talk to her. Make her see it's important."

"It won't be easy."

"Nobody promised it would be easy," said Buchanan. "This whole thing, it's not easy."

"I'll look in on her." Flo got up, leaned and kissed Buchanan on the cheek. "You're a nice big slob," she said, then went out the door.

"Oh, yes. A big slob is right." He checked the revolver, put it in his pocket and went out the back way. He walked down to the bank and deposited the money with the single cashier, a youth named Horace Weevil. He went into the office and Sam Dade was looking through a mound of papers.

"Hi, Sam. Got anything?" asked Buchanan.

"Maybe a glimmer."

"Walt know about it?"

"I hope not." Sam was nervous. "I wish the auditors would hurry. I need some expert advice."

"Somethin' to do with Walt?"

Sam said ashamedly, "And with my father, I'm afraid. There are gaps in the bookkeeping. They date back before dad was killed."

Buchanan said, "Never mind the dead. It's the livin' we got to worry about."

"I know." Sam bit his lip. "When I'm sure of anything I'll let you know. I have a feeling I'm getting close. Real close."

"Get to me before you get too close," Buchanan told him. "You know what happens to folks in Culebra."

He went back to the hotel and changed his clothing. He

had been up since dawn and needed a nap but he decided there was too much going on at the Silver Dollar to allow him that luxury. He went back to the saloon.

He returned the revolver to its place in the desk. The party was still going. Strangers passing through had got into the spirit of things and Flo was kept busy at the piano. Brannigan had hired another man to help behind the bar. Cook and the Krags were at the same place, drinking beer, saying little, watching. Were they waiting for someone or something? Buchanan would have given a lot to know.

He went behind the bar and filled a pitcher with ice and water. He climbed the stairs again and tapped on Addie's door. A groaning small voice bade him enter.

She was on the edge of the bed, her head in her hands. "Some snake stole my bottle," she whimpered.

"Here, try this." Buchanan put the pitcher in her hands. She drank thirstily. Swallowing hard, she asked, "Now can I have my bottle?"

"You really want it?"

"I don't wanna think."

"Sooner or later you got to."

"Make it later." She put a piece of ice in her mouth and crunched it.

"You talk tough. But you're not tough."

"I wasn't tough," she corrected him.

"You want us to nail Hempel, don't you?"

"I'll do it myself if somebody else don't."

"We need help," said Buchanan. "We need Hagen."

"Don't talk about him to me."

"Listen Addie. Hagen's the marshal. If we could get him to do what we want, it'll lead to Hempel."

"Hempel's his deputy."

"You know better than that. You know Hempel and Frey were pushed on him."

"Yeah. He's the kind. People can push on him."

"Maybe you could help us straighten him out, show him what he's go to do."

"Not me. Not never."

Buchanan said softly, "Dick would want it that way. You think it over."

She stared at him. The tears came. He dipped his kerchief in the water and gently washed her face.

"You just hang in there. I'll send you some food. And you keep thinking of what I said. Flo'll be up."

"Flo's an angel. Flo believes."

"That's right." What Flo believed was that she understood men and Buchanan hoped she understood women as well, particularly this poor girl.

"Flo believes Dick and me were gonna get married."

"Sure, we all believe that." It was a kindly prevarication, he thought. "Just you rest and eat and keep thinkin'."

"I don't wanna think. I want my booze."

"Later, maybe," he promised her.

She turned from him, lay face down on the bed, and began to sob silently.

Buchanan left the room. He could not deal with womanly hysterics. He motioned to Flo, who left the piano and threw kisses to the admiring men.

"She's still a bit drunk," Buchanan said. "Take her up some more water and I'll send out for grub. Don't let Hagen see her until she straightens up a little, at least."

"Okay," she said. "Anything you say, sir."

She went upstairs with the water. Buchanan went to help the bartenders who again were being swamped with orders. He wondered if Dick Coverly deserved such a party on the occasion of his burial. Unless something happened to clear up the mystery of Culebra he might never know.

The night wore on with loud sound and milling men. Cook and the Krags vanished. It occurred to Buchanan that he had not seen Hempel nor Frey that day. He went out for a breath of air and saw a light burning in the office of the marshal, behind which was the jail. He walked down and saw Hagen sitting with his feet on his desk, a shotgun conveniently placed at his right hand. He tapped on the door and Hagen peered out, then admitted him.

"Didn't want you to be startled," Buchanan said. "You look loaded for bear."

Hagen said, "The damn deputies. One of the mines has a payroll coming. They went to guard it. I got to watch the prisoner."

"You going to sleep here?"

"With all the hullabaloo in town I reckon to." He was offhand about it. His mind was still somewhere else.

"Addie's feelin' a bit better but I wouldn't see her until tomorrow if I were you."

"Yeah. Right. Seein's Dick's scarcely cold. I got no sense when it comes to Addie."

"It happens, they tell me," Buchanan said.

"There's somethin' about her—she'd just a country kid. Coverly—well, he was good to her, I guess."

"She might've done a lot worse," said Buchanan. "He wasn't one of your bully boys."

"He was right decent, seemed to me," confessed Hagen. "This whole crazy business, I just don't understand. Hempel got clear, of course. Nothin' anyone could do. And Walt Store and Jody Teller back them up."

"There'll come a time when you'll have to make your move," Buchanan cautioned him once more.

"Maybe I'm scared of them. Frey with those sly sneers, his quick gun. Hempel with the guns and the Bowie. I never did like a knife. Backstabbers carry knives. Maybe they've got me buffaloed." He faced Buchanan. "Like you say, I'll have to face it out with them one of these days."

"One of these days soon," Buchanan said.

"There's a reward for our friend in there," Hagen said. "When I collect it, I may pull out. Get the hell away from all this."

"We'll see." Buchanan waved a hand at him and left the jailhouse. Hagen was a puzzle to himself as well as to others, he thought. A lot depended upon his actions and it was a long shot that he would come through.

People, he thought, people is a critter. That's what his father used to say. He walked past the bank which was dark. He turned and went back to the Silver Dollar. It was

78

after midnight and the crowd had dwindled to the precious few who could wassail until dawn.

Flo was at the far end of the bar having a drink. "I'm so doggone tired I can't make it without little helper, here," she said. "Addie is sleeping, mainly because I slipped her a bit of laudanum in her booze."

"She start to drink again?" He was disappointed.

"She did, indeed. When she stopped bawlin' she began sopping it up. I'm afraid we're going to have a little problem with our Addie."

"Poor kid, she's not too bright to begin with."

"Too true," she said. "I'm afraid Hagen won't be gettin' any glad smiles from the woman he loves."

"He loves her, all right. Never saw a worse case."

"Can't we close the joint?" Usually perky, she was slumped against the bar. "Buryin' and celebratin' has got me worn down to a nubbin."

He said, "Give 'em an hour. We got to be true to the owners, you know."

"The lousy bank."

"Don't forget our percentage."

"You think we'll ever collect? Or will that bank go broke on us?" She flashed her gold tooth and took the drink back to the piano. She played slow pieces very lightly, her knuckles and fingertips aching.

Buchanan ordered himself a nightcap. He nursed it, aware that he, too, was weary. He had been up since dawn, riding; then to the burying, then the fight in the bar, now this vigil over a bunch of drunks. It had not been a fruitful day, either. Now he had to worry about Hagen and also Addie.

He finally decided to close up. He gave Brannigan the signal to call time, went to Flo. She got up from the piano with alacrity and he walked her to the foot of the stairway.

She said, "Nobody'll have to rock me to sleep. Unless you'd take the job?"

"I'll find you a rock," he offered.

She said, "A lousy joke. Goodnight, Buchanan."

"Sleep tight." He watched her go up the steps. For a little girl, she had plenty of curves in proper places. One day she might be sorry she teased and tempted, he thought. That would be another day.

He went back to the hotel and fell into bed. He was sound asleep in thirty seconds.

Chapter Six

There seemed to be a drum beating. Buchanan turned over in the bed and groaned. Instinctively he knew that he had not slept long enough. He opened one eye. Light shone through the drawn windowshade. He turned over and buried his head in the pillow.

The sounds started again. Now, half awake, he recognized them for what they were. He rolled out of bed, naked, grabbed for clothing. He jammed on his boots and took up his rifle. He threw up the shade and the sash. He leaned out of the window, looking down toward the bank.

He saw the backs of riders going furiously out of town to the south. They wore long linen dusters. In the street someone was shooting after them. Buchanan leaned his cheek against the stock of the rifle, sighted.

Then he put the rifle down, pulling back into the room. They were out of range. He buckled on his belt and carried the rifle down the stairs. People were running into the bank. Buchanan followed. There was no sign of Marshal Hagen as he went past the jail.

Inside the bank all was confusion. The young teller, Weevil, was nursing a bleeding head. Dr. Dudley was telling people to stay out of the office.

Walt Store, pale and shaken, was saying, "They came in when we opened. Three of them. I think there were one or two outside. I don't really know. They held me under a gun. Sam wouldn't open the safe. They . . . they shot him."

Buchanan asked, "So you opened the safe?"

"I value my life and that of young Weevil more than money," Store said. "Where is Marshal Hagen? Why doesn't someone go after them?"

Men were saddling up. There were shouts and confusion in the street. Buchanan shouldered into the office and looked at young Sam Dade. The doctor was working on him. There was too much blood on the floor.

Sam opened his eyes. He saw Buchanan and tried to speak. The doctor frowned but Buchanan leaned close. Sam's eyes flicked, his tongue ran between dry lips.

"Buchanan . . . Frisco . . ."

"Sure, Sam. Take it easy."

"I mean it . . . San Fran-cisco . . ." The voice trailed off.

The doctor said, "He shouldn't try to speak."

Buchanan looked down at the young man. "Reckon it don't make any difference now, Doc. I seen too many this way."

He turned and walked out into the street. Someone was coming from the marshal's office, waving his arms and yelling. Buchanan ran in that direction, thinking of the young life ebbing away on the floor of his office in the bank. He had liked Sam Dade from the start. A hard anger began to build inside him now.

Tim Hagen was sitting at his desk. He was holding his head. Buchanan cleared the office.

Hagen said hoarsely, "I was asleep. Someone slugged me."

"What time was it?"

"An hour or so ago. I tried to get up—a man can't be knocked out that long."

Buchanan reached and opened an eyelid, peering. "They poured a few drops into you, while you were out. See it in your eyeballs."

One look at the cells told him the prisoner had flown. He went to the door and examined the lock. There were scratches which might or might not indicate forced entry into the office. There was a cot on which Hagen had been sleeping. Otherwise nothing seemed to be disturbed.

Hagen was saying, dazed, "They robbed the bank? Did somebody say they robbed the bank?"

Buchanan said, "There's a posse ridin' out. Won't do a bit of good, but let 'em ride."

"I've got to go with 'em. It's my job."

"You couldn't ride a hobby horse right now. You didn't see nor hear anything?"

"No. I had to get a few winks, bein' alone here." Hagen's voice was furry and uncertain.

Buchanan examined the marshal's skull. There was a soft spot behind the ear.

"Now that could've been managed with a blackjack," he said. "And leave it to prizefight people to know about knockout drops."

"Blackjack . . . didn't you say somethin' about a blackjack?" Hagen was trying to clear his head. He started up but sank back into the chair.

"That I did." He started to put things together in his mind. "Sandy Folger. The Krags. Cook. They all come into town at once. I better talk to Walt Store. You just stay here and wait until the dope wears off, you hear? We'll ride out later."

"Later?"

"I never yet saw a posse catch anybody with a lick of sense," Buchanan told him. " 'Specially a bunch of town people. Later we'll take a look at a couple places."

"I don't understand." Hagen held his head in both hands.

"I'll send the doctor over to give you somethin'," said Buchanan, heading for the door. "You stay still until I get back here."

On the street he almost ran into Flo Dockerty. She was holding a handkerchief to her eyes, walking blindly toward the hotel. Two men were carrying Sam Dade's body out of the bank on a shutter.

Buchanan took hold of the girl's shoulders. "I'm thinkin' a prayer for him right now. But we've got work to do. Flo. Get back to the hotel and see if you can learn if Cook and the Krags left early. Then watch out, keep that gun handy. We're comin' down the stretch on this pretty soon."

"The poor kid," she sobbed. "He liked to have fun. He was just a nice young fella who wanted to have a good time."

"You're right. So do like I say before some other nice man gets killed. Like me."

She shivered and looked up at him. "I'll be all there, Buchanan. I'll be there."

"I know you will." He gave her a little shove toward the hotel.

He strode into the bank. Walt Store was shaking off questions from investors. He dragged Store into his office and locked the door. Store wrung his hands.

"Why didn't you go after them, Buchanan?"

"Reasons. Tell me, how many were there?"

"Four of them. Four . . . I think."

"Yeah. You said three, maybe one outside. You notice anything about 'em that would help?"

"They wore masks and those long linen dusters. They must have copied the James Gang. They had a sack. They put the money in the sack."

"How much money?"

"I don't know exactly. More than enough to wreck the bank if they're not caught. Can't you do something? Didn't Sam hire you to do something?"

Buchanan ignored the questions. "You couldn't have a notion who they might be?"

"Why . . . no. They were—well, they were all sizes. Tall, short, medium. The voices were muffled by the masks. No, I couldn't identify any of them."

"You haven't asked about the marshal, where he was or anything," Buchanan said.

"Didn't he ride out with the posse? What do you mean, I haven't inquired? His job is with the posse."

"He couldn't make it," said Buchanan. "Somebody turned his prisoner loose and conked him good."

"He allowed a bank robber to escape? Buchanan, can't you see the connection? It's as plain as day."

"Looks that way," said Buchanan. "Well, reckon I'll take a ride out."

"Now? It's too late."

"Oh, sure. It's late all right. How some ever, Nightshade needs his exercise. Nightshade, that's my horse. Gets fat standin' around Jody's stable. I'll let you know if I find anything."

He left Walt Store staring after him as though the banker thought him demented. He did not believe Store thought any such thing. He went back to the marshal's office and Hagen was buckling on his gun, pale but determined. Buchanan waved him outdoors and they walked toward the livery stable.

Hagen said, "Doc said there were four of 'em. Could be Folger and the three men you know."

"What have you heard from Hempel and Frey?" asked Buchanan.

"Why, nothing. They're on that job for the mine."

"Uh-huh. Look, I got dressed too quick. You go get our horses ready. Be right along."

He went across to the hotel. Flo was in the lobby, all traces of tears removed.

She said, "They're all upstairs sleepin' off their jags. Nobody saw any of 'em go out."

"Yeah. That makes it Hempel, Frey, Folger, and one more."

"What? How do you know?"

"I don't exactly know. But it's a real good guess, I'll bet on that. And I'll bet sneaky little Spike could get in and out and no one the wiser."

"But he's upstairs now. I had the boy use his key and make sure of it."

"Didn't figure him to be ridin'. He's no horseman."

She stared. "You mean he just went around the back way and came to the hotel and went to bed? After the getaway?"

"When I saw them, they were outa range. Hard to tell with the sun and me barely awake and all. But I only saw three riders. Walt Store said three, then he said maybe four."

"Didn't anyone else see them?"

"Oh, sure. Could have been four—then all of a sudden, three. See what I mean?"

"But Hempel and Frey? They're on a payroll job."

"So I heard."

"You don't believe it?"

"I'm open to convincin'."

"You think you know the answers?"

"Not all of 'em," said Buchanan. "Gettin' there, yes. Will you take over the saloon for me 'til I get back?"

"Where are you going?"

"Just a little ride," said Buchanan. "My hoss, y' see. Needs exercise."

"All right, don't tell me. Go ahead, Get yourself killed but don't let me in on anything."

"Nothin' to let you in on. Not yet. Watch the bartenders. And don't put any more money in that bank."

"Not likely," she said, grinning, her tooth gleaming gold in the sunshine streaming into the hotel. "Have a nice ride, you liar."

He went over to the stable. The horses were saddled. Hagen was talking to Jody Teller in the yard.

Buchanan said, "Hi, Jody. Where were you when the guns went off?"

"Sick." He was wearing a nightshirt which he had stuffed into his pants. His feet were thrust into slovenly slippers and he had not shaved. His sharp features were blurred, haggard. "They got Sam, did they?"

"Old man Dade, his son, Coverly," Buchanan ticked them off. "Nice quiet little town you got here, Jody."

"It was quiet," said Jody dully. "It was goin' along right good."

"Somebody threw a wrench into it," Buchanan said. "Puts you to wonderin'."

"Like what?"

"Like who's next?" Buchanan swung aboard Nightshade and rode onto Main Street with Hagen. The marshal was still listless, not quite himself, but he remembered something. He put up a hand and Buchanan reined in.

"Got to tell Jackson to telegraph the sheriffs about Folger."

They tied up at the telegraph office. Buchanan was curious since he had never spoken to the operator, a small balding man named Sime Jackson. The marshal gave his instructions and Jackson shook his big head.

"This town is going to hell," he said. "One damn thing after another."

Buchanan suddenly asked him, "Any word about the payroll Hempel and Frey rode out to guard?"

Jackson looked bemused, then said, "You mean the

Apache Mine payroll? It got held up, didn't come through. The deputies are on their way back to Culebra."

"But they reported to the mine?"

"Must have. We got word from the foreman up there."

"When did you get the word?"

"Last night before closing. About nine."

"And how far is the Apache Mine?"

Jackson looked at Hagen, who said, "Oh, about forty, fifty miles west of here."

"West, eh? Not north?"

"No, good road westward."

Buchanan said, "Let's take that ride."

On the street, Hagen said, "You think Hempel and Frey could've got back to town and . . . No, they couldn't."

"Why not?"

"Well, forty miles, maybe more." He paused. "But they had time, didn't they?"

"More than enough time."

Hagen said, "Do you know somethin' I don't?"

Buchanan sighed. "Hagen, that's somethin' you can tell better than me."

"You don't trust me, do you?"

"I wouldn't trust my grandmother in this mare's nest."

Hagen fell silent. Buchanan ran it all over in his mind again. The pieces fell into place. The only problem was that he had no proof.

It was a bright, sunny day, indifferent to tragedy. They rode to where Buchanan had found the farmhouse and turned off. Hagen was surprised but Buchanan forged on. They dismounted in the yard and Buchanan insisted upon putting the horses in the barn. Hagen, mystified, did as he was told. They entered the house.

Again Buchanan went directly to a stove. This one was still warm as had been the other. "Figured this was closest. There's an empty line cabin out yonder. But anyone could hide here, let the posse go by on the main road where nobody can track three horses real good. You need an Indian to pick up that kind of trail, anyway."

"How do you know the robbers were here?"

"I don't. I don't know a thing." He reached into the firebox. The ashes were soft, there was nothing left unburned to examine. He rummaged through the entire building. He returned to the kitchen, disappointed. He leaned against a wall and wondered why a fire had been made. Paper, he thought, damaging documents. Too bad they had done such a good job of destruction.

His eyes wandered. There was a table and two rickety chairs on either side. Someone had sat there while the papers burned.

He leaped forward so that Hagen, startled, hopped across the room. He picked up one of the chairs and put it carefully on the table. He took out his Barlow and opened a sharp blade.

Hagen said, "What the hell? You whittlin' at a time like this?"

Buchanan cut carefully into the splintered wood. He extracted a bit of material and put it on the table. Hagen bent to look closely at it, drew in a quick breath.

"That's the stuff linen dusters are made of!"

Buchanan said, "Ain't it, now? You see how it was done?"

"They came here first and burned some papers. Then they rode in and hit the bank. It was backwards, like."

Buchanan said, "Right. Then they hit shale out yonder and left no trail. Then they doubled back. Folger is long gone with his share of the loot. Or he's hangin' around for a bigger payoff."

"Bigger? They cleaned out the bank."

"Did they?"

"People were yellin' it all over town. Walt Store told 'em the bank was cleaned out."

"He did? Now, that's funny. He was refusin' to say how much was stolen when I saw him."

Hagen said, "I'm still lost."

"Uh-huh. Think of it this way. Hempel and Frey double back. They get a picklock to open the office and hit you on the head and slip you some knockout drops. They spring loose Sandy Folger. They come out here and pick up the linen dusters and burn some papers—papers from the bank, let's say. Then they go in and hold up the bank and kill Sam Dade. Could we guess the papers they burnt were seen by Sam? That Sam was on to some monkeyshines around the bank?"

Hagen thought a moment, "What you're doin', Buchanan, you're layin' this at the door of Walt Store."

"Am I?"

A bullet slammed through a window and spatted into the wall. Buchanan seized Hagen and threw him to the floor.

"Stay here. Watch and be ready with your Colt. Odds are he's got a rifle."

"But who? Who's out there?"

"If it ain't Folger then I wouldn't know. When you shoot, pull the trigger twice each time. I want him to think we're both in here."

"Where you goin'?"

"I'm goin' out to play," said Buchanan grimly.

He went to the far side of the house, keeping his head low. He climbed out of a window in a bedroom. He ran for a copse of live oaks, keeping the house between himself and the rifleman.

If he had his own long gun he could climb a tree here and possibly get in a shot. On the other hand, he would rather have a prisoner. He needed the answers to a lot of questions. He thought he knew the answers but they had to be corroborated.

He made his way through the trees and the brush. He could move like a smaller man and with less sound than most. He remembered his earlier ride, the contour of the countryside. Shots sounded. A puff of smoke arose from the rockpile he had noticed on a hill a hundred yards from the house. It was a natural fort.

He had to make a detour. He had to chance that the bushwhacker would not leave his safe position and charge. He did not believe anyone would attempt either a sortie or a scout against two guns. He worked his way to higher ground inch by inch.

Now it became even more difficult. He wanted to get high gun on the rifleman and take him alive. He came around behind the rocky little hill. He dropped behind a heavy growth of sage and considered the situation.

There was no cover on the hill. It was about twenty feet

at the summit. The only way he could get there was to climb. He waited for the sound of shots, taking a breathing spell, making himself smaller, his mind turning over.

He thought of Sam Dade, who had been honest with him, whom he had liked from the start in San Francisco, now lying dead, not yet thirty, not yet fully matured. He thought of Dick Coverly in his grave holding secrets which may have solved the mystery of Culebra; and of the girl, Addie, who mourned for Coverly while clutching a bottle of whiskey.

He thought of Jody Teller whom he had known and liked for so many years, now ill and nursing the private snake in his gut. He thought of the deputies and of Walt Store and he thought about the man up there on the hilltop.

It had to be Sandy Folger because none of the rest of them would risk recognition in a showdown like this. He had been brought in for a purpose and he had remained out here, lying low, for another purpose. Cook and the Krags, also brought in for reasons, they were not gunmen nor horsemen. So it was Folger, a recognizable type, an outlaw, a thief and a murderer.

Yet Folger had seemed an ordinary man, rather a decent sort, amiable in the bar, smiling, unperturbed. Buchanan had seen a good many of them, riders gone wrong for one reason or another. He had mingled with them, had drinks with them, and he had faced their guns and they had faced his.

But always he asked himself, why? He was truly and deeply a peaceable man. Because guns were the tools of the frontier he had mastered the use of them. He did not believe in them, he abhorred killing, he thought that if guns were prohibited the frontier would be a better place to live. He foresaw a day when this would be true—and knew also that it would end a way of life when every man stood on his own feet and went his own way—Buchanan's way. He did not dwell too long on this line of thought.

It was amazing how much could go through a man's head in a few seconds, he thought. He examined the sun-swept bare hill for the quickest way to the top. There were loose stones scattered carelessly about, no clear path that he could detect. He shifted carefully behind the mesquite, straining for the sound of gunpowder exploding. All his old wounds ached for the moment. He knew the next few moments might add to them or lead to sudden death.

The shots came with sharp suddenness, first the rifle, then two quick returns by Hagen. At the first sound Buchanan started up the hill. He was six feet four and weighed well over two hundred pounds but his long legs carried him with startling speed. Rocks rolled beneath his boots. The sun was hot upon him.

He saw the figure of the man, saw the rifle barrel. He shouted, "Sandy, give up!"

The man behind the gun fired. Buchanan's hat flew from his head. He raised the revolver. He fired offhand, hoping to hit a leg, a shoulder. His foot slipped on a round stone and he went to one knee, knowing he had missed, bracing himself for the man's second shot, feeling that he must take it and again try his aim.

The man seemed frozen to the hilltop. Then he straightened and threw his rifle from him. He toppled, turning over and over. He rolled down the hill and came to rest at Buchanan's knee.

It was Folger. He was already dead. He lay quite still, staring at the sky, at the blinding sun he would not see again. He looked very young and clean for a moment, then he sank into himself and was a bundle of clothing and bones and flesh, nothing, a thing inert. Buchanan sighed.

He called out, "Hagen. You got him."

Hagen came to the bottom of the hill. He looked up and said, "I was scared he'd got you."

"A near thing. He maybe would've. Got to thank you." Yet he wondered for a moment. Hagen had fired quickly. Did he think Buchanan was already dead? Did he make certain Folger would not talk of what had happened in Culebra?

He told himself the thought was unworthy, that Hagen had saved his life. "Bein's you're the law, maybe you'd better search him."

Hagen plodded up the hill, sweating, holstering his revolver. He knelt and went through the pockets of the fallen man. He turned up nothing but an old leather folder with pictures facing each other and a smeary letter between them, tobacco and papers, matches, a clasp knife and four silver dollars.

Buchanan said, "Maybe a money belt."

Hagen fumbled gingerly beneath the shirt, nodded, unbuckled the belt and drew it out. He unlaced it and took out some money. He ran the money through his fingers.

"Less than a thousand dollars," he said. "If they made a square divvy, four of 'em that would be less than four thousand. But Walt was yellin' that they cleaned the bank."

Buchanan looked at the blond young marshal. "What do you think now?"

"It just don't make sense. Walt workin' against his own bank. It can't be."

"So it can't be." Buchanan let it drop. "You for takin' this poor fella in? Or buryin' him here?"

"Buryin' him?" Hagen did not understand.

"Well, if we bury him, you won't be involved."

Hagen thought it over. "They'll think he just ran off."

"Right."

"And if we bring him in they'll know I went after him and we got him."

"Right."

Hagen wiped his hands on his pants. "Buchanan, I think you got me all wrong. I'm wearin' this badge. Maybe I'm kinda slow, maybe I don't understand everything that's goin' on. Maybe I been too wound up in Addie and all. but we're totin' this corpse into town. It's my job."

Buchanan said, "Best, then, we catch up to his horse."

"Right."

Hagen, he thought, could not be one of them—whoever they were—and he thought he knew exactly who they were now. The marshal might still be an unknown quantity, an uncertain young man befuddled by events, unsure of which way to jump, but he was not an ally of the other forces.

It had to be Store and the deputies, Hempel and Frey. But the reasons for their actions were not quite clear. There was no actual evidence upon which to act. If the marshal was slow in moving, Buchanan could not be quicker. Sooner or later the entire matter would come before a court of law. Buchanan wanted to be mighty sure of his facts in that case. He helped Hagen carry the still warm body down the hill to the stable. They went to look for Folger's horse. Both men were silent with their thoughts.

Chapter Seven

Hagen turned over the money found upon Sandy Folger to Walt Store. Buchanan was with him to verify the sum, he maintained.

Store said, "I'm naturally upset. The scoundrels, shooting Sam down like that."

Buchanan said, "How much did you say was stolen from the bank?"

"I didn't say. Certainly the man—Folger? He did not receive his share."

"So?"

"Perhaps the posse will recover the bulk of the money." Store was agitated.

"You own the bank, now. Right?"

"I will be in charge until the law takes its course. Daniel had no other offspring. Poor Sam." He wiped an eye.

"Yeah. Poor Sam. Poor Daniel, Poor Coverly."

"Coverly?" Store shrugged. "A cheat."

"A dead gambler who owed the bank. You don't want to tell how much was stolen this time?"

Store frowned. "This time? There was no other time. Really, Buchanan. Bank business is private for good and sufficient reasons. I have no more to say."

Hagen started to leave but Buchanan held his ground, leaning against a wall, looking at the banker. Store's fingers drummed the desk top. His lips were thin, twisted.

Buchanan said, "Sam hired me to look into his father's murder. Is the bank good for this?"

"Well . . . I mean, I had no knowledge. Just what do you mean, Buchanan?"

"Two-thousand dollars if I brought in the answer. Is it worth that to you?"

"Why, no. Not now." Store spread his hands, leaving them flat on the desk to control their restive flexing. "After all, I did not hire you. We have the marshal and his deputies to maintain law and order in Culebra."

"How about the Silver Dollar?"

"You're doing a good job, there, I must admit. I . . . the bank needs every dollar of income." He hesitated and Buchanan knew he was plotting, sitting there, working it out in his mind. "I think you might stay on as manager."

"All right," said Buchanan. "I'll do that."

"Then, if you'll excuse me. . . ."

"One more question," said Buchanan. "The fifty thousand that old Daniel Dade was carrying. Where was he going with it?"

"I don't know!" Store was vehement. "It's a mystery." He stopped dead, bit his lip. "How did you know? Oh, of course. Sam was wrong to tell anyone, you must realize. The bank is under stress. I have to think. Something must be done."

"The bank does business with the mines. There's two spreads out yonder that need tenants." Buchanan shook his head. "If I was to have investment in this bank I reckon I'd be workin' on those properties. I'd be talkin' to the mine owners. I'd be tryin' to make everyone chip in to help."

"Are you telling me my business?"

"Nope." Buchanan lapsed into his Texas drawl, innocent, simple. "Last thing I am is a businessman. Just thinkin' out loud."

"I'd rather you did your thinking aloud at the Silver Dollar," Store said. "I must be alone to think things out for myself. And the bank."

"Right," said Buchanan. He lifted a hand and walked out of the bank. Hagen followed on his heels.

They walked to the office of the marshal. When they entered Hempel and Frey were lounging. Hempel was behind Hagen's desk, his face ugly. Frey sat on a chair, his legs crossed, smoking a cigarette. Neither stirred.

Buchanan watched Hagen. The marshal was nervous, moving to the door which led into the cells of the jailhouse. The silence built tension in the room.

Hempel said in his gravelly voice, "So you got Folger."

Hagen said, "We got him."

"Shot him for breakin' out."

"Shot him in self-defense," said Hagen, but his voice was not hearty, convincing.

"He jumped the two of you?" Hempel sneered. "Didn't think much of you, did he?"

Buchanan could brook no more of this insolence. He said mildly, "While you were gone, Folger helped rob the bank. Or didn't you know?"

Hempel turned, deliberate, scornful. "Nobody asked you, did they, Buchanan?"

It was a familiar spot, a forced showdown, Buchanan thought. He shifted so that Frey was in his line of vision. He had left his gun belt at the hotel after returning to town, as was his lifelong habit. Aggression, always, had to be met with aggression.

He said, "You know somethin', Hempel? I don't like the way you handle yourself. Too biggity."

Frey moved his right hand closer to the butt of his gun. Buchanan could also see Hagen. The marshal was pale and silent, it was a crucial moment for him.

"You know somethin' your own self? I don't like you no better." Hempel came from behind the desk. The Bowie knife hung between his shoulder blades beneath a loose hickory shirt. "You keep buttin' in all the time."

"Somebody ought to," said Buchanan. "Like when you and your miserable little pardner set up Dick Coverly."

"You accusin' us?" Hempel was girding himself for action.

"I wouldn't say nothing like that." He was caught in the middle between them. He didn't have a chance. He glanced at Hagen and saw the marshal's hand move, saw his jaw harden. He was unobserved, the deputies thought they knew their man, knew Hagen dared not interfere.

Hempel gave no warning. He dove forward, punching for the groin. At the same time Frey jerked his hand and Hagen drew with speed, throwing down on the little deputy, his decision made, a final step from which he would never be able to escape.

Hempel intended to double him over, then butt him in

the face. It was a good maneuver. It had been tried before by men who knew Buchanan's prowess and thought they had the answer to offset it.

Buchanan twisted toward Frey, making certain that the little gunslinger would not draw. He caught sight of Frey's eyes, full of hatred, directed at the action rather than at Hagen. At the same split instant he struck down, bringing both hands to the nape of Hempel's neck.

Hempel clattered to the floor, roaring. His right hand went to the lanyard which suspended his Bowie. He came up with the foot-long, shining razor-sharp blade in his hand.

Before anyone could move or speak, Buchanan was upon his man. He grabbed for the right wrist. He got his hold and spun. Hempel's boots flew in a circle.

Frey tried to duck but was caught by a heel and went down clattering. Hagen jumped upon his desk and pointed his revolver downward at the fallen man. Buchanan swung Hempel again, then let go of him.

Hempel went against the door leading to the cells. Buchanan was on him like a cougar. One wrench and the Bowie came free.

Buchanan tossed the knife to Hagen and said, "Hang onto this for a minute."

Hempel, strong as an ox, gathered himself, shaking his head in blind rage. He swung a fist. Buchanan caught that in his left hand and chopped a right to the face. Blood spurted. Hempel tried to clinch.

Buchanan let the big deputy come in close, then wrapped his arms around the thick body. He straightened. Hempel's feet cleared the floor. Buchanan squeezed. Hempel's legs threshed, he tried to squirm loose, his face began to bulge. Buchanan applied more pressure. Hempel's breath came in short gasps.

Buchanan turned him loose. Hempel staggered in a circle, blood streaming, eyes blank.

Buchanan opened the door of the office. He grabbed the deputy, and spun him. He applied his boot to Hempel's rear. He propelled his victim into the bright sunlight before all of Culebra. He sent him sprawling into the dirt street. He followed him, picked him up.

Very deliberately, Buchanan slapped Hempel with his left hand, holding him with his right, rattling his teeth and what were left of his senses. People stared, children and dogs whooped in the street. Buchanan administered one more cuff alongside the jaw and let go. Hempel sank to the edge of the wooden walk, half-conscious, cursing, and completely whipped.

Across the street Walt Store looked through the window of the bank. He saw Buchanan staring at him and vanished. Flo Dockerty came from the Silver Dollar, grinning, her tooth shining in the sunlight.

Buchanan said distinctly, "People won't be scared of you now, Hempel. You know that, don't you?"

Hempel coughed up more blood and did not reply. He managed to get to his feet and stagger into the office. Buchanan went to the door. Hagen was a bit shaky, but he held the gun steady on Frey.

Buchanan said, "Good time to fire your deputies, Hagen."

"Fire 'em?"

"You're the boss. You saw them try to set us up for a kill."

"Kill?" Hagen swallowed hard. "Uh—yes, that's right."

"Never find a better time," Buchanan insisted.

Hagen coughed. Then he said, "Hempel. Frey. I'll take those badges."

"You didn't hire us and you can't fire us," said Frey. His eyes blazed with hatred now.

Buchanan said, "You want me to take 'em from them, Hagen?"

Frey snatched at his badge, tore his vest taking it off. He flung it on the desk. "You ever touch me, Buchanan, you'll roast in hell that day."

Buchanan went to the dazed Hempel and removed the star. He said, "This one don't even know what's goin' on. If in fact, he ever has."

Hagen said from a dry throat, "How about you puttin' on one of them, Buchanan?"

He shook his head. "Me, I'm manager of a dive. Wouldn't look right. But if either of these two randies give you any trouble, just let me know."

Frey said, "You'll know when I turn my wolf loose, Buchanan. You'll be the first to know."

"Better get your pardner out of here," Buchanan suggested. "And be awful careful not to touch that hogleg you're so proud of. A fella can get hurt playin' with firearms."

Frey supported the bulk of Hempel. They went across the street to the bank. Buchanan watched them stagger inside.

"Birds of a feather," he said. "Walt Store, sittin' there, givin' us all that jabber. Guilty as sin, all of them. Plus Cook, the Krag brothers—and others."

"Yeah, maybe," Hagen said, still shaken by what had occurred. "But where's the proof?"

"I still got to talk with a friend of mine," said Buchanan. "I still want to hear from him."

"You think Walt will try to make me take Hempel and Frey back again?"

Buchanan looked at him. "You know, sometimes I worry about you. You know enough, maybe too much. But you fiddle around, first one way then the other. It's growin' up time in Culebra, Hagen. It's fish or cut bait. It's live or die. Make up your mind, time's runnin' short. I'm a peaceable man but I'm losin' patience."

He went out to join Flo Dockerty. She took his arm and while the town looked on in amazement and awe, paraded him to the Silver Dollar.

They stood at the bar and Brannigan served cold beer, wagging his head in wonderment. Flo giggled.

"Didn't believe he could do it, did you, Brannigan? Told you. I know men."

"You was bitin' your nails," Brannigan said. "But it wasn't Hempel scared me. It was Frey. I seen him get that iron of his'n out. Like a damn snake. Bang!"

"Hempel was fast enough when he got Coverly," said she. "How can Frey be quicker than Hempel?"

Buchanan held up his beer. "Culebra. Nice, quiet town."

"It useta be," said Brannigan.

"I been in hot places. Cowtowns. Outlaw hideouts. El Paso. I been in the Tenderloin in New York City. That's real mean. So here we are in little old Culebra and we got murders and shootups and fights and robberies all over the place. It don't figure."

Flo said, "It happened. I bet you're hungry."

Buchanan drained his beer. "Whenever I get time to think I'm hungry."

"I got some sandwiches and milk and apple pie."

"Lead me to 'em." He cocked an eye at her. "You do know some things about men, at that."

He followed her into the office. She was a right smart little gal, at that, he thought. Sometime he would have to tell her about it.

Now he said, eyeing the thick sandwiches and the cold milk, "Got to tell you. The bank won't pay off on our deal with Sam."

"Never thought they would," she said.

"You could take the stage in the morning."

"Where to?" She showed him her grin again.

"Any place but here."

"I pass."

"It's goin' to get worse."

"I know."

"I'll split our take here at the saloon with you. But you'd be smart to duck out."

"No. I'd be smart to stick with you."

He thought it over. "Because you're in so deep?"

"Maybe I couldn't get far enough away from the deputies. Or Walt Store," she suggested.

"There's that," he admitted. "You still got that gun?"

"Not on me, but I got it."

"I'd hate to have anything happen to you, Flo."

"Whatever happens, I can take it."

"And you know all about men."

"I know about men," she agreed. "Eat your sandwiches."

Chapter Eight

By nine o'clock the Silver Dollar was doing a land office business. Men came to Buchanan and told him they'd been waiting for months for someone to take the measure of Hempel. The tables were busy and Flo was singing and playing.

Buchanan went upstairs. Addie was sleeping again. The room was stale with the odor of booze. He went back to the barroom and told Flo he was going to look in on Jody Teller.

He had not seen his old friend all day. When he returned from the ride and stabled Nightshade the hostlers had shrugged and denied having laid eyes on Teller. The time had come for a talk and Buchanan was determined to have it out in the open between them. He believed that Jody knew enough of the truth to throw light on what had been happening in Culebra and why.

The house was dark, which was unusual since Jody habitually left a lamp burning low in the kitchen. Buchanan let himself in and fumbled until he found the lamp. The wick sputtered and threw a weak gleam. Buchanan carried it through the other rooms. He found nothing, went back to the kitchen and sat a moment, pondering.

The change in Jody had occurred between the time Buchanan left Culebra for San Francisco and his return. Always a quiet, easygoing man who talked a lot, he had shown a different side, as though something was worrying him. And this was before Buchanan had discovered the body of Daniel Dade. There was a meaning here, Buchanan thought. It was something he had to learn.

The house was filled with an empty stillness. The lamp sputtered. The oil was low and the wick turned brown.

Buchanan blew it out and at that moment he heard the shot.

He ran out the back door. The house was a couple of hundred yards from the stable. He heard Nightshade whinny and ran harder. A dark figure hurried away and was lost in deep shadows. Buchanan gave chase but realized it was impossible to catch anyone in the dark back ways of the town.

He turned back to the stable. Again he had to fumble for the lantern he knew was suspended from a peg in the wall. He struck a taper and applied it to the lantern. He held it high.

Jody Teller lay in the middle of the stable floor. Blood seeped from beneath his body. Buchanan brought the light closer and saw the wound, in the chest directly over the heart. Jody was dead.

Buchanan put the lantern down and made certain that life was extinct, his finger gentle on the pulse of Jody's neck. He remained motionless for a moment, hunkered down, silently praying for the soul of his friend.

He set the lantern on the floor of the stable. He searched the pockets of the dead man. There was no money, which was odd, since Jody liked money and carried it all the time. Indeed, it was his love of money that had brought him here, Buchanan believed. Yet there had not been time for robbery, so swiftly had the killer fled.

Inside the vest was a pocket. From it Buchanan took a folded piece of ruled paper, recognizing the handwriting of Jody. It was a note addressed to him.

> *Tom, Old Friend, I've got in too deep. This here is too much for you or me. Better get out of here. They want me to . . .*

The writing trailed off as if Jody had decided not to finish, or was interrupted—or uncertain about the warning. In any case it pointed to the reason for his murder. "They" had wanted him to do something and he had refused.

Buchanan found a horse blanket and covered the corpse. Someone else could clean up the blood, he was

102

weary of blood and of killing. He had never held life cheap and most people, he knew, felt the same. Gunslingers were criminals in his book. To survive he had learned to cope with them but he was truly not a violent man. He went to Nightshade, wishing the horse could talk, could tell him who had met with Jody in the dark of the stable. He calmed the horse, whispering in its ear.

He went out and down the street. People came and went, the night people. The Silver Dollar was full of the sound of revelry which spilled out into the cool air.

Hagen was in his office, staring at nothing. He seemed numb, as though he had abandoned thinking. He looked at Buchanan and asked, "You seen Walt?"

"No."

"He stopped by. Told me he was keepin' the deputies on as shotgun guards because of all the happenin's."

"Sure, that figures."

"Said they were mad at you. Said you better watch out."

"Now ain't that decent of him?"

Hagen shifted his feet. "You sure took care of 'em."

"With your help."

"Walt said they'd be after me, too."

"Scared you, did he?"

"Not that much." Hagen shrugged. "They're mean enough to bushwhack anybody. Could happen any time."

"Somebody just did it to Jody. He didn't have a gun on him."

"Jody?" But Hagen did not seem surprised.

"In his own barn. Face on, in the heart."

"Jody was in somethin' with the bank."

"He had all his money in the bank. He set great store by his life's savin's."

Hagen was silent. Then he asked, "How's Addie?"

"Drunk," said Buchanan bluntly.

"Mournin' that tinhorn."

"Flo's watchin' over her." He eyed the marshal. "Still thinkin' on Addie, are you?"

"Once started, you don't stop," Hagen said. "I better get Doc Dudley and see to Jody."

They met Dr. Dudley coming out of the telegraph office. He was a balding man of middle age, continually harassed by the demands upon his time by the sick and by a wife and four children.

"What is it now?" he demanded.

They told him. He shook his head and went with them to the stable. By the light of the lantern he examined the body.

He said, "Point blank. See the powder burns?"

"That's murder," said Hagen. "He wasn't armed."

Buchanan said, "Murder on top of murder. How do you figure it, Doc?"

"Evil in the air. I believe you are of the opinion that Daniel Dade was murdered?"

"There was sign," said Buchanan. "Nothin' to be proved."

"I just sent a telegram to San Francisco," said the doctor. "I am considering a move. The atmosphere of Culebra is deadly. The bank . . . what little I have is in the bank."

"San Francisco," said Buchanan, half to himself. "Things turn on the place." He remembered Sam Dade's last words, which had been wandering in the reaches of his mind. He had met Sam in the bay city, it had all really started there with Flo and the Krags and Coco and Konecke.

"It is civilized, at least. Culebra was civilized, or near to it, a fine, prosperous, burgeoning town," said Dr. Dudley. "Life becomes different overnight. I have to think of my family."

Hagen had not been listening. "Doc?"

"Yes?"

"Is there anything you can do for a . . . a person . . . who's been drinkin' too much?"

"A drunk?"

"No! A . . . a lady. Addie Hale."

Dr. Dudley said, "She is not a drunk. I will see her if you wish."

"I'll pay for it," said Hagen. "Poor gal's in the dumps. If you could give her somethin'?"

"After I have seen the undertaker, I'll try to help."

"I'll get Harrison," said Hagen eagerly, seizing at hope. "I'll get the coroner's jury and everything."

"Very well," said the doctor. "Mr. Buchanan?"

"Okay, I'll take you to her." He was thinking of San Francisco. It had become some sort of key, he believed. He had to put it together with what little he knew and what he guessed.

It kept rolling in his mind as he sent Flo upstairs with Dr. Dudley, as he surveyed the crowd for strangers or tough drunks, and checked the poker tables and the wheel. He was still thinking San Francisco when Dr. Dudley came downstairs and departed.

"How did it go?" he asked Flo.

"First he made her throw up. Then he gave her somethin' to make her sleep. She's like a poor little wet kitten up there right now."

Hagen had just come into the saloon. Buchanan beckoned to him, said, "You can go up and take a look now if you want."

Hagen looked at Flo. "You think it's okay?"

"I'll go with you."

They went up the stairs. Buchanan went into the office and thought about San Francisco. Once more he went through the few papers left by Dick Coverly. There was nothing.

Flo came in and sat down. "She asked us what happened to her, where she had been. At first I thought she was goin' to cry again. She said we all smelled like death. Then she saw Hagen standin' there like a big booby and she actually tried to smile at him. Can you imagine? So I told her he'd sent the doctor and she thanked him."

"Then what?"

"Then I blew out on a breeze. At least she's talkin' to him. Hope she remembers when she wakes up."

"Hope is the word," said Buchanan. "Hagen, he needs some hope. He's walkin' a tightrope. Store's got him bamboozled. He can't figure Store ruinin' his own bank."

"Or robbin' it?"

"Either way," said Buchanan. "If business was so good, why should he go to break the bank he owned?"

"Beats me."

"You ever hear of Store in San Francisco?"

"No. Sam mentioned him. Sam was scared of him and of his old man, y' know. Wait!" She squinted, screwing up her face. "Somethin' about the stock exchange. Sam said there was millions to be made in minin' stock. You know, the Comstock Lode, all that. Only it goes up and down like an elevator, 'cause I looked into it with another gent I useta know."

"Stock exchange." There was a welter of sound from the bar. He sighed. "Another night for the dead."

"Dead? Who?"

He told her about Jody. She listened, her face dull.

"Too much blood," she said. "Addie's right. There's the smell of death on the town."

"They're all from the bank. It would seem now that Store is next. Only I don't believe it'll be him."

"If he lives it proves we're right. He's behind it all."

"And will get away with it. Unless we come up with somethin'. And soon. Real soon."

"Because we're next," she said grimly. "And maybe Addie."

"Not to mention Hagen."

"How far can they go?"

"They've gone this far, they got to keep on," said Buchanan. "Have you seen Cook and the Krags?"

"No."

"San Francisco," Buchanan said. "All from San Francisco."

"It does seem like that."

"Tell me, Flo. You know men. What do you make of Walt Store?"

Without hesitation she answered, "A cold fish. Not interested in anyone, much less women. He's concerned only with himself. All tied up in his guts, so there's no way to get at him."

"And smart."

"Real smart," she agreed. "Guys like that, I've known 'em. They sometimes work themselves into a corner and can't find door nor window."

"Which is just the way I feel right now."

Hagen came into the office, calm, relaxed. "She's asleep. She said I could be a brother to her."

"Ain't that grand?" Flo snorted.

"Well, maybe she'll get used to me after awhile."

"After a long while," Flo told him. "Dick ain't cold yet."

"Now, Flo," said Buchanan. "It's men you know about."

"Well . . ." She relented. "I have heard of fallin' in love on the rebound. Like you got to turn to somebody."

"I hope so." Hagen sighed.

The three of them went into the saloon. Cook and the Krags were holding court. Local men listened.

"Sounds like you didn't have no trouble 'till this Buchanan come to town," Cook said.

"Never did think of that." It was a rider, Buchanan saw, one of the posse which must have returned empty-handed and sore.

"Maybe youse'd better look into it. Wasn't he inna game when Coverly got kilt?"

Buchanan interposed, facing Cook. "You were speakin' of me?"

Spike Krag reached inside his coat. Buchanan picked him up as though he were a rag doll and sat him on the edge of the bar where he wriggled in raging impotence.

"Seems like I have to teach you manners, little man," Buchanan said to him.

His brother made a move. Buchanan rapped him on the knuckles with his fist. "Stay out of this. Want me to hit you again?"

Spike was yelling, "You lemme down off'n here, you big lummox. I ain't scared of you."

"Somethin' you oughta learn," Buchanan said. "Fear's a mighty helpful feelin' sometimes. You just sit there with your blackjack for a minute."

Cook said, "Here, now, Buchanan, you got no right . . ."

Buchanan interrupted. "You were just saying as how none of these killin's happened until I came to town."

Everyone was silent, listening. Hagen moved away from the bar. Men moved restlessly.

Buchanan said, "Nobody robbed a bank, either, before

107

I came here. Nor killed good friends of mine, namely Sam Dade and Jody Teller. I just want to tell it to the world. Nobody else gets killed until I find out what's going here. That's a gamble I'm taking. Nobody else, you hear?" He paused, then said, "Until I get my hands on those behind these doin's."

He stepped away and Spike fell off the bar and into his brother's arms. Cook's face was red. The man to whom he had been speaking slunk into the crowd.

Buchanan said, "Drinks on the house," and turned away. They would have to come after him now. He had made the statement for them to hear and word would get to them, to the deputies and to Store and to whoever else was involved. That's the way he wanted it.

He walked through the crowd and out of the saloon. Jody, he thought, had been about thirty-five. Too young to die. A man who had been good in his time, had done good for others. They would be burying Jody tomorrow.

It was time to buckle on his gun again, to carry it with him against all his principles. He believed it brought trouble . . . But trouble had already been carried to him. More would come. He did not want another death, he felt guilty that Daniel Dade, Coverly, Sam Dade, and Jody had died.

Chapter Nine

They buried Jody Teller.

That evening Addie Hale came downstairs into the confusion of the inevitable wake. She was quiet and pallid but she smiled and was able and willing to serve drinks. Flo played and sang. Buchanan wandered among the people, the name of the bay city still on his mind.

He was watching the poker game when it hit him. He walked swiftly to the door and across the street to the telegraph office. Jackson, the operator, was reading a newspaper.

Buchanan said, "Would you answer a few questions?"

"What about?" He was a sober little man.

"About telegrams. You keep a record?"

"Certainly. That's part of my job."

"I'm interested in messages sent to San Francisco."

"I can't let you in on any secrets, you know."

"It might be important. Too many people are gettin' killed in Culebra."

Jackson rose to the statement. "You know what? I've been thinking about that. Really worrying."

"You got money in the bank?"

"I have, if it wasn't stolen. I've been worryin' about that, too. The wife has been talkin' a whole lot about that."

"Yeah. I'll bet she has. Well, tell me goin' back a ways, did anyone from the bank send messages to, let's say, a broker in San Francisco?"

"Mr. Store."

"I see. Could you dig out any of those messages?"

"I got them all. The bank always is sendin' wires to San

Francisco. But mainly Mr. Store. Only, you see, they're in code."

"Code?" His heart sank.

Jackson smiled slyly. "Code. But there's no code I can't break. I'm a telegrapher. I study codes."

"Well, now, that's fine. So you know what's in those telegrams?"

"I sure do. Can't let you see them, though."

"Okay if I guess?"

"Well, will it help? I mean all the doin's, killings?"

"It may help."

"I suppose I can't keep you from guessing."

"Let's see—Mr. Store was investing in stocks havin' to do with the Comstock Lode. Using the bank's money, of course."

"The bank's money? But that's not legal."

"Just why I'm curious," said Buchanan.

"The Comstock—H'mmm, let me think. Yes, that's right. Mining stocks."

"You imagine he was makin' money?"

Jackson hesitated. "You sure this might help everything?"

"I'm sure I need to know."

"I know I was wrong, Mr. Buchanan. But I didn't use the information for my own gain. I did check, out of curiosity, when I saw the San Francisco papers."

"And had Mr. Store bet on the wrong horses?"

"You knew."

"I guessed. Now tell me, you do have those records?"

"Like I said."

"And you can translate 'em?"

"I can."

"Just hold onto them," Buchanan told him. "The proper people may want to subpoena them."

Jackson said, "You're not going to mix me up in anything, are you?"

"Nope," said Buchanan. "Not me. I'm just tryin' to unmix this town of Culebra."

"I sure hope you can do it. Jackson was concerned. "It was such a nice town. I sure want to stay here."

110

"Hide those records," Buchanan advised him. "If anyone else should ask, tell 'em you burned them."

"I'll do that, Mr. Buchanan. And best of luck."

He left the telegraph office and went back to the Silver Dollar. Addie was still on the job, looking better. Flo was playing a southern song, "Crawdad," and some of the customers were grouped around the piano singing the repetitive words, *"Sittin' on the ice 'till my feet get cold, watchin' that crawdad in its hole, honey, sugar baby of mine . . ."*

Hagen was watching, his face serious. When he saw Buchanan, he hurried forward.

"Store sent word. He wants to see you and me at the bank."

"Wouldn't be surprised. We better talk first."

They went into the office and Buchanan said, "Must have seen me comin' out of the telegraph office. Set down, im."

The marshal seated himself. He looked uncomfortable, apprehensive.

Buchanan said, "To start in with, I've been look for fifty-thousand dollars taken from old Daniel Dade when he was killed."

"Store said . . ." Hagen stopped. "I'll be damned!"

"Yeah. Where would Dade be goin' with fifty-thousand dollars up in the Black Range? That's had me stuck. Now, if he didn't have the money, why did he get killed?"

"To get him out of the way."

"Out of Store's way. Now, if Store had been bettin' the bank money on the stock market and losin' it and Walt agreed to meet him up in the hills and explain all—or for any other reason he might find—how about it?"

"How about what?"

"Was Store in town that day? Hempel? Frey?"

"I just don't know. I didn't see any of 'em that day until late."

"Yeah. That's what I thought. So let's stick to the fifty thousand. It's not in the bank or Sam would've found it. Sam did learn that Store was in the market, that's what he meant when he tried to tell me about San Francisco when he was dyin'. Make sense to you?"

"It makes sense."

"Okay. Now, I'm no detective, but a Pinkerton once told me detectin' was mostly common sense. Let's say Coverly and Jody Teller knew somethin' was wrong but had to go along with any lie Store told 'em for fear of losin' their savin's—in Coverly's case the saloon. Still with me?"

Hagen heaved a deep sigh. "You're right."

"You knew it?" Buchanan eyebrows shot up.

"I knew Store was into the market," said Hagen miserably.

"And you kept quiet?"

"Everybody was gettin' wise." He gulped. "Buchanan, I got to tell you. Store's got me where the hair is short."

Buchanan nodded. "That's another matter. You actin' the way you been, off agin, on agin Finnegan."

"I . . . was in trouble once. Store knows it."

"Prison?"

"Store got me out. He sent for me to come here. I could send me back if he wanted to."

"A pretty kettle of beans," said Buchanan. "No wonder you been skittery."

"You wouldn't hold it against me?"

Buchanan said, "Sho, who ain't been in jail? Thing is, can you make up your mind to buck Store? All the way?"

"I got to." Hagen's fists clenched. "I gave you a lot of palaver about wearin' the badge. But now it means somethin'. I never held with killin'. And Addie—maybe I got a chance with her, give her time. I got to go your way."

"All right. I'll believe you. I'll keep an eye on you, mind, but I'll believe you for now."

Hagen said, "If I could get clear with Addie . . ."

"First things first. Now about the fifty thousand, which is the difference between a broke bank and a goin' bank. Where you reckon it is?"

"I got no notion."

"Well, Jody didn't have it. Jody just began to crack up. I could see it—and there was the note he left. So . . . that leaves Coverly. But they had to kill him for fear he'd crack. Or maybe just because he did have it and they didn't trust him, come to think on it."

"Coverly? You mean it's here in the saloon?"

"Did a bit of readin' in my time. Fella name of Poe. Edgar Allan Poe. Wrote a story called 'The Purloined Letter.' Thing about the letter it was almost in plain sight. Store, he's an educated man. Figured a man like me wouldn't ever read a story."

"But where can it be?"

"Haven't even looked. My common sense has been too doggone common, which is mainly the trouble with common sense." He grinned. "Call Addie in here."

Hagen went into the saloon. In a moment he returned with the girl in tow. She looked a bit weary, but she had regained color and was able to smile shyly at Buchanan.

He said, "You ever done spring housecleanin', Addie?"

"Well, sure. What do you think I am?"

He let the question go by. "Would you do me a favor? Would you start upstairs and clean like you would at home?"

Her eyes popped. "Tonight?"

"Sooner than that. Check every nook and cranny."

"It sounds crazy to me."

"Every inch, you understand?"

"Well, if you say so." She looked uncertainly at Hagen, who nodded vigorously to her. "You and Flo and Tim . . . you been awful nice to me."

"Okay," said Buchanan. "Get goin'." She left, still puzzled. He said to Hagen. "All right, let's go and get fired."

"Fired?"

"Jody's dead. Nobody else to keep us in our jobs. Store's now the boss. Boss of the bank. Boss of the town. Right?"

"I didn't think of it that way. He sure is."

"He's got Hempel and Frey and Cook and the Krags to back him up. Lot of muscle there."

"But what can we do?"

"Nothin'," said Buchanan. "Just keep on gamblin'."

"Gambling?"

"That we'll be alive tomorrow," said Buchanan. "Should we dance?"

"All the business houses on the street were darkened

excepting the bank. The door was open. Hagen lingered but Buchanan took his elbow.

"They won't shoot us offhand. They're afraid we might get in a couple ourselves. They like the easy way. Like killin' people who are unsuspectin' or unarmed, remember?"

He opened the door and walked into the bank. Store was in his office. Hempel and Frey were leaning against the wall. Hempel looked as though he had been thrown from a horse and stomped. Frey wore his hat cocked to one side to allow room for the lump where Hempel's boots had struck him.

Buchanan eyed them and asked innocently, "You boys been in an accident or somethin'?"

They growled but did not speak. Store cleared his throat. A nerve twitched in the corner of his mouth but he spoke quietly and deliberately.

"I know all about what happened in the marshal's office and I consider it a disgrace."

"Well, your boys will play. I'm a peaceable man, but they're too rough."

Store said, "I'm unhappy with both of you."

"Now, that is too bad." Buchanan pretended concern. "That really hurts me."

"In a word, because I represent the council in this town, I demand that Hagen turn in his badge, this moment."

Hagen said, "That's okay with me."

Store took the badge. He extended it to Frey. "You will be the town marshal."

"Leastways he looks better'n his partner, there," Buchanan remarked.

"As for you, Buchanan, I am also the sole representative of this bank. We now own the Silver Dollar. We no longer want you in charge there."

"You got your 'we's' mixed up with your 'I's' haven't you?" Buchanan shrugged. "However, you're the one to decide."

"I have decided. Hempel will take over at once. And I want those women out of there, also."

Hagen stirred at the implied slur upon Addie and Flo but Buchanan nudged him to silence, saying cheerily

114

"Well, the boss might be ever so wrong, but he's still the boss."

"You have some money coming to you," Store said. "I have no desire to cheat anyone. How much do you think I owe you?"

"Oh, a couple hundred," Buchanan said carelessly. Then he brightened. "Tell you what. I'm gettin' to be a gamblin' man, hanging around the Silver Dollar. Why don't we have one last poker game after the place closes?"

"I don't really think . . ." Store paused and his brow cleared. "You mean just those who are here?"

"If it's all right with you," Buchanan said. "Easy come, easy go. I'll back what you owe me with a few hundred more."

Store relaxed. "I am glad to see you taking it this way, Buchanan. Why not a friendly game before we part?"

"Oh, me, I'm peaceable," Buchanan told him. He looked again at Hempel and Frey. "Ask them."

He steered Hagen out before more could be said. They walked back toward the saloon and he was chuckling aloud.

"What's so funny?" Hagen was aggrieved. "I thought you were gonna that bank apart. I was ready to help."

"Funny? I'll tell you what's funny. A man who so worships the dollar that he'll risk everything to cheat somebody out of a few hundred."

"Yeah, and they'll be ready to shoot. Frey and Hempel. Remember what happened to Dick Coverly."

"That's just exactly what I'm rememberin'," said Buchanan. "Just how it was done."

"You forgettin' about those Frisco thugs?"

"I wish I could forget 'em." They were a real threat. He wondered how Store had come across them. It was probably through gambling. The one thing he knew about Store was that the man could not resist a gamble. It had led to all the trouble in Culebra, this sickness. It had led to death for too many men.

"Just the two of us." Hagen shook his head. "I don't mind a gamble but the odds are too big this time."

"Nothing's that big. You want Walt Store on your trail the rest of your life? You want to live fearing he'll send you back to prison?"

"I don't want to have to kill him to stop him."

Buchanan sighed. "I never want to kill anyone. That's for the hangman. Thing is, we seldom get our druthers in this world."

"The girls—Addie—might get hurt."

"They shot Addie's man. You got to keep that in mind. He was good to her, remember that, too."

"He didn't marry her!"

"She thought he wanted to. She believed. People got to believe, have faith. You have to bear with 'em."

"I know it's goin' to take time. But she treats me better this last day or so. Since she got off the booze and all."

"Hold that thought," said Buchanan.

"I'll try." He inhaled deeply. "A gamble. A gamble for just about everything in my life. Okay, Buchanan."

They had come to the Silver Dollar. They pushed through the swinging doors. Cook and the Krags were still at the bar, talking in low tones to Brannigan.

Spike yelled, "Hey, look at the law feller. He lost his damn tin!"

The remainder of the crowd stared. Hagen faced them, no longer flinching, staring back at them. Nobody spoke.

Buchanan was watching Brannigan. "Set 'em up. Then you're fired."

"You can't fire me!" Then Brannigan turned red, white, and purple.

"Ah, you know. So you are the spy. Knew there was one around."

Brannigan blustered. "I know my place and my rights, too."

The customers began to leave. They had seen far too much trouble in town and now something more was brewing. Buchanan went to the piano where Flo had stopped playing and was waiting for him.

"We're fired," said he.

"Uh-huh. Now what?"

"Let's take a look upstairs."

"It's gettin' to be close, right?"

116

"Closer than that."

Upstairs, Addie had a towel wrapped around her head. Her freckles shone and she looked no more than sixteen. There was a small pile of rubbish on the floor of the hallway. She leaned on a broom, frowning. Hagen went to her.

"Dick's room," Addie said. "It was dusty." She bit her lip, looked at Hagen. "It wasn't so bad as I thought it would be."

"Just take it easy," Hagen urged her.

"Is this all you found?" Buchanan indicated the rubbish.

"That's all." She flushed. "Empty bottles."

"Forget that. Let us look in your room."

"It's cleaned up now."

"Somethin's been bothering me about your room."

They all went through the door. The bed was tightly made, the furniture squared in orderly fashion. The door of one closet was open, her clothing neatly hung in place.

Buchanan said, "What about the other closet?"

Addie frowned. "Why, I never looked into it. Dick . . . Dick told me not to."

"I been studyin' on that closet," said Buchanan. "That's why we didn't start takin' Jody's place apart."

"It's locked," Addie said.

"That's why it come to my mind. Let's see about that lock."

He examined it. Then he tried the knob. The door was stout. He gripped tighter. He exerted the enormous strength of his arm and shoulder.

The doorknob came off in his hand. Hagen's eyes bugged out. Even Flo was astonished. The door swung open.

The closet was empty.

Buchanan said, "A locked door and nothin' behind it? Don't make sense, does it?"

He bent his head and inserted the upper half of his body into the emptiness. He ran his hand around the pine boards of the interior. He stepped back and pondered. He looked at the other closet.

He said, "They look different."

"This one's deeper," said Hagen.

"Uh-huh." Buchanan knelt and examined the back of the second closet. There was a small aperture into which he could insert his fingers. He reached in and pulled.

The back wall of the closet came forward. He lifted it and small nails screeched in protest. Between the wall of the next room and the closet was a space wide enough to contain two saddlebags. He pulled them out. They were nondescript, unidentifiable until he looked very close and saw the initials "D.D." inscribed with a fine pen.

"That would be Daniel Dade," he said. He opened one. Stacks of bills and a canvas sack that clinked of gold came to his grasp. "Fifty thousand?"

He delved into the other bag. He pulled forth a linen duster. Beneath it there was more money.

Addie said with infinite sadness, "Dick must've put it there."

"He knew about what they did to Dan'l Dade. He had to. Which is maybe why he acted like he did. Which has got to be why they killed him, either because he knew too much or because he didn't like what was goin' on."

"But he didn't trust me!" Addie wept on Hagen' shoulder. "He could've told me."

"And get you into it?" Buchanan shook his head. "Coverly had his decent side, we all know it."

"I don't care. He should've told me." She was inconsolable. Hagen put a tentative arm around her as she sniveled.

"Startin' with Daniel Dade," Buchanan ruminated. "He must've got desperate when he found out Store was gamblin' away the bank money. And Jody Teller. Same thing. Sam, he began to catch on and sent for the auditors. So Store had to get rid of him. Now somebody has to clean up and clear out before the auditors get here. Which is right now."

Flo said, "How come only one duster?"

"Dick was dead by the time it was put in here."

Buchanan replaced the saddlebags. The door was broken beyond compare but he saw no reason for concealment.

Hagen asked, "Shouldn't we get that loot outa here?"

"Where would we put it?" Buchanan squared his shoulders. "Why do you think I set up that poker game?"

"You're buckin' big odds." Hagen paused, then said, *"We're* buckin' big odds."

"People have been murdered. There's a town out there with ordinary, plain people in it. The town's in danger, of more killin', or goin' broke. Is it worth a gamble?"

"It's worth it," said Hagen. He grinned. "It's nice knowin' there's a stake that big. Thanks Buchanan."

"Don't thank me. Pray a little."

Addie sobbed, "I don't know what you're talkin' about. I'm discombobulated altogether."

"You tell her," Buchanan said to Hagen. He motioned to Flo and they went into Coverly's room next door. "You still got that gun?"

She whipped up her skirt. The weapon was too big for ˄r shapely slim leg but she had attached it with elastic so ʌat it was securely in place.

"Mighty pretty," said Buchanan.

"You took note!" She showed her golden tooth.

"The day I don't enjoy a pretty leg is the day I'm dea˄ ˄ grinned at her. "And that could be soon. So you keep ʌ̖e gun handy."

"And not even a profit in the gamble," she mourned. "Sam's gone, our jobs are gone."

"But we still got the gamble."

"You and me and Hagen against that mob?"

"It was just you and me before," Buchanan reminded her.

"You believe Hagen'll come through?"

"I don't know how good he is." Buchanan was serious, now. "That remains to be seen."

She sat with her knees crossed. She wore a long, full gown, cut low at the neck. Her pert little face screwed up in thought. "Brannigan."

"If you can manage to unload that shotgun of his, it might be a big help."

"I'll manage it. He's no brave man, anyway. Just a bartender. He was snoopin' around. I thought it was just, you know, nosiness."

"They had to keep somebody around to watch over the money. No one left to suspect but Brannigan."

"You think he knows where it is?"

"Nope. But he could report anything amiss, you see?"

"Cook and the Krags."

"Dangerous people," Buchanan admitted. "Quick hands. Fightin's their business."

"It would be nice to have your man Coco around."

"Coco could be a help."

"Hempel and Frey. Quick guns," she said.

"And Store. A mighty mean man no matter how you look at him."

She said, "Buchanan."

"Yes?"

"The fifty-thousand-whatever dollars."

"Uh-huh. I know what you mean."

She laughed without much humor. "We could get outa . We got the guns, they don't know we found i. We could get clean away from here."

"No doubt about it."

"Was a time I might've tried it alone." She patted bulge beneath her gown. "With your gun."

"You couldn't hardly manage it."

"Oh, I wouldn't try for it all. Just enough to pay me for my stay in Culebra."

Buchanan said, "You want to try it now?"

Her eyes became large and round. "You mean you wouldn't stop me?"

"Nope."

"I don't believe it."

He said, "Way I see it, better you should be out of here tonight. You could get hurt. I know you wouldn't run, I know that about you. So . . . better you should take a bit of money—which is nothin' compared to bein' hurt. Or killed."

"Oh." She looked hurt before the event. "I thought maybe it was because you like me."

"Why, girl, I liked you right from the start, when you stood there in that fancy Frisco hotel in your pretty dress and grinned at me."

She beamed. "You did not!"

120

"I sure did. And like I say, you're okay. You're a purely standup gal."

"That's the trouble." She made a monkey face.

"What's the trouble?"

"Purely," she said, her eyes darting fire. "Too damn much purely."

"Now, Flo. I'm a long rider. Well, almost. I'm always ridin' long and windin' up in trouble I don't want. I'm no kind of a catch for a gal."

"Don't talk me out of it."

He was startled. "Out of what?"

"Buchanan, when this is over I'm goin' to attach myself to your coattails and just try and shake me loose." She bounced across the room and kissed him hard on the mouth. He got up from the chair and she clung on, again dangling her legs, now laughing and enjoying his strength.

He said, "Look here, this is serious. We got to get crackin'."

"Just what's on my mind," she gurgled.

"Not you and me. All of us." He plucked her loose and set her on the floor. Then he bent and kissed her on the nose. "You're the best, Flo. The very best."

"If you'd only let me prove it," she wailed.

He propelled her out of the room into the hall. He thought, oh, my goodness. First Coco, now this one. Why can't they let a poor, peaceable wanderer alone?

They heard Hagen's voice from the other room. "If we get outa this we can at least be friends, Addie. Right?"

"I'd like that." Her voice was small and sad.

"You don't belong in a saloon. Look at you. You look like a nice young lady keepin' house."

"Do I?"

"You always looked like that to me."

"I didn't have any house. I didn't have anybody 'till Dick picked me up."

"Dick's gone. You need somebody. A man."

"I reckon every girl needs a man."

Flo pinched Buchanan so that he jumped.

Hagen said, "If you just gimme the chance."

"I was wrong about you." Her voice was soft. "I see now how good you can be."

"You wasn't wrong. I was mixed up. I got a lot to tell you some day."

"About bein' in prison? Dick told me."

"He had it from Store, then."

"Yes. He had it from Mr. Store. I'm . . . I'm sorry."

"Don't be sorry. Buchanan straightened me out. I know what to do, now."

"But what can you do against them?"

"Try," he said. "You can always try."

"Hempel," she said. "I know maybe Dick wasn't straight with me about everything. But Hempel's got to pay."

"He'll pay."

"I'll feel free if he does. I'll feel like the last link of a chain is broke."

"You'll be free. If we get through it, you'll be free."

"Then I'll listen," she said softly. "A girl needs a man."

Buchanan coughed. Flo was pinching too hard. Hagen and the girl came out close together, hands clinging.

Buchanan said, "Addie, you get dressed for travel. We're all fired, understand? Flo, you put somethin' on top, a shawl or somethin', like you're ready to go, too."

"I've got a jacket she can wear," said Addie.

Buchanan said, "Come on, Tim."

They went to the head of the stairs. They stopped, listening. There was no sound from below. The party was over.

Buchanan said, "Have your gun ready just in case they decide not to gamble and waylay us."

"That's right, they're the law, now."

Buchanan went first, Hagen staying back to give each of them room. The barroom was deserted excepting for Store, Hempel, Frey, Cook, the Krags and Brannigan.

Buchanan said, "Well, looks like the gang's all here."

The Krags and Cook were at the bar. The front doors were closed and locked on the outside, beyond the swinging doors. There was only one light, a chandelier above the table, reflecting its brilliance downward upon the green of the cloth. Hempel and Store were opposite one another, already seated, with Frey on Store's left. That put Buchanan between Hempel and Store, Hagen between Frey and

attempt to help Flo take the shells from the shotgun. He had to manipulate the cards in the face of a trio of dishonest dealers.

Talk about gambling. Here was the biggest of his wild and woolly career, right here at the poker table.

It was odd about poker. The game might be planned as a farce, a means to an end, but true poker players always became caught up in it as soon as the cards began to slither around the green cloth. The sheep and the lamb were identical, each felt the full fascination for the gambit.

Brannigan was now talking to the San Francisco bunch. Flo edged in, then drew back as the bartender drew more beer for the trio.

The first ace fell to Frey. He took the deck, gave it a long shuffle. Then he proffered it to Store for the cut. The banker complied. Frey took back the deck and swung it to original position so that the cut did not matter. Buchanan sat back and waited. It was plain to see that they were wasting any time.

glanced at his cards. He had three tens. He waited Hagen.

"Open for ten," said Hagen.

"Play," said Hempel.

Buchanan said, "Sorry. Can't play these."

Frey stared, then a film came over his eyes and he bit s lip. Store put in ten dollars. Frey did not raise.

Hagen said, "I'll take two."

Store said, "One'll do me."

Frey thought a moment. His own draw had been ruined when Buchanan dropped. He held the deck loosely in his hand. Buchanan never took his eyes from it.

Frey said hoarsely, "I'll take—uh—three."

Hagen said, "Check to the one card."

"Bet ten." Store seemed a bit confused.

"I'm out," said Frey.

"Call," said Hagen.

Hempel thought a long moment. He might be adept at dealing, but he was not strong in the brain, Buchanan believed.

"I'll call," he finally said.

Hagen said, "Three big ones." He showed aces.

"Good by me." Hempel glared at Frey. But the hand had not been designed for the big deputy. It was supposed to go to either Store or Frey, Buchanan knew. Hagen raked in the small pot.

"Better than a sharp stick in the eye," he said. He took up the deck to deal.

Suddenly there was a rattling noise at the door. A drunken voice shouted, "What's goin' on in there? Why can't a man get a drink?"

"We're closed," shouted Brannigan.

"You Irish whelp, you can't shut me off from me booze." It was a belligerent miner just off shift and thirsty.

Brannigan went to the door. "Kelley, I told you we're closed. Now go home to your wife."

"I'll do no such of a thing until I get me drap." Kelley shoved at the door, kicking and hammering.

"Lemme handle this," said Hempel. He rose from t[he] table and started for the door. Every eye was upon him.

Flo made her move. She ducked down behind the [...] Buchanan said loudly, "Yeah, let the law handle it, [...] nigan. You got no respect for the law?"

He rattled the gold coins in front of him to cover [the] click of metal when Flo broke the gun and removed [the] shells. Addie was sitting quietly at the piano and he wished she could break into a tune like "The Battle Hymn of the Republic," loud and strong. Hempel was opening th[e] door.

The big miner came hurtling in. Hempel hit him behind the ear. He dropped and Hempel dragged him out, shouting after him, "And stay out, all of yez!"

Buchanan's heart stood still in the silence of the saloon. Then Flo reappeared, cool and serene, grinning, flashing the gold tooth. Buchanan breathed again. One obstacle had been removed.

Meantime he had not missed a whispered exchange between Store and Frey, who were also taking advantage of the interruption. Both were looking askance at him. He maintained his grin as Hempel came clumping back to the table.

"Can we have a game, now?" Buchanan asked.

126

Hagen put in his ante and dealt. Watching him, Buchanan had to suppress a chuckle. Somewhere along the line, possibly in the long hours of his prison term, Hagen had learned to deal bottoms better than Frey or Hempel. None of the others showed the least suspicion as the cards flew around the table.

Buchanan did not even look at his cards. Hempel said belligerently, "Open for twenty."

Buchanan said mildly, "I'll take a chance."

"You're betting blind?" demanded Store. "Fool. I raise twenty."

Frey said, "I'll see that and raise another twenty."

Hagen shrugged. "I call."

Hempel crowed. "Just right for me. Raise fifty!"

Buchanan said mildly, "Now I better take a peek."

He edged his cards. Hagen had taken no chances. He had dealt Buchanan a pat straight flush to the king.

"What do you know?" Buchanan asked no one. "Just ~ky at cards, unlucky in love."

~lo coughed at the bar but no one noticed.

Buchanan said, "I raise a hundred."

Store's mouth pinched in. Greed shone from him. "I will raise that a hundred."

Frey said, "I drop."

"Too steep for me," said Hagen.

Hempel's high spirits had diminished. He peered across at Store. "I call."

"Cards, if any." Hagen held the deck loosely in his left hand. He seemed to be enjoying himself at last.

Hempel took two. Buchanan said, "I'll play these."

Store did not flinch. "One to me," he said.

Hempel was confused. "Check to the pat hand."

"Two hundred," said Buchanan.

Store inhaled. "And two hundred."

"This is crazy," said Hempel, ditching his cards.

"And two hundred." Buchanan's stake was getting low.

Store said, "No pat hand is worth that much, unless— no! I don't believe it."

"You lack faith, Mr. Banker," said Buchanan. "That's a sin, lacking faith. You can always call me."

Store said stiffly, "I shall certainly call."

"Got about fifty left over. That's all you can raise me," said Buchanan, deliberately baiting his victim.

Store slapped down the money. "I raise."

Buchanan stuck in his last gold coins. "Call because I got to."

"Ha! Four aces!" said Store.

"Like I said." Buchanan dropped them one at a time. "All pink, to the king and right in a row."

"I still do not believe it!" Store's voice was faint. The man could scarcely bear to see his money change hands.

Buchanan stacked his money. Hempel was the dealer. He made a try at arranging the cards to suit himself. He was pretty good, too, but not good enough. When he gave the deck to Hagen to cut he had it stacked but Hagen slid out the middle, made a pass and completely spoiled whatever Hempel had been trying to do. Buchanan was enjoying himself to the hilt.

He looked at his cards and saw two pairs, aces eights, the gambler's hand reputed to have been held Wild Bill when he was shot in '76. Disbelieving in Buchanan pushed in chips.

"Open for fifty."

Store, still suffering from the previous hand, played along. Frey played. Hagen raised. Hempel mumbled at lack of success in framing the hand and also put in hundred dollars, hoping, probably, to extricate a card to help his hand.

Buchanan, following the odds that two pairs were fine before, but not after the draw, called. Store met the raise. Hempel came in, scratching out the money.

Buchanan stole a look at the girls. Cook and the Krags had moved down near the open end of the bar, still talking with Brannigan who was now close to his shotgun. Time was running out, Buchanan thought, with the cards going totally against the conspirators.

Then he saw that Addie had changed to a straight chair and moved it closer to the table. He wished he could signal her to move back to comparative safety but her gaze, filled with hatred, was upon Hempel.

He said absently, his concentration on the game broken, "One card off the top."

Hempel dealt him a card. Store took one. Frey took two. Hagen took one. Hempel took one. Buchanan riffled the edges and almost gave it away. Hempel in his bungling had dealt him the third ace.

He said, "Bet two hundred."

Store said a bit too eagerly, "I call that."

Frey gritted his teeth and also called. Now that the cheat was broken they all had to stay in to protect the others. Hagen looked at his hand.

"Raise two hundred," said he blithely.

"That's damn brother-in-law poker!" roared Hempel.

"Watch your language," Buchanan said. "Play or drop."

"Don't you tell me what to do, you stinkin' sidewinder!"

Addie hitched closer to the table. Buchanan leaned back, hooking a foot around a leg of the table. Frey _uched. Hagen inched his chair back and the trio at the _ gathered themselves for a charge if need__.

Store said firmly, "Play your cards, Hempel."

The big man threw them down with furious emphasis. "Damn if I play."

_tore said triumphantly, "I tap you both for what you _ve on the table."

"Fair enough." Buchanan watched the banker count _heir money, Hagen's and his, and match it dollar for dol-_r. The big gambler again, he thought.

Finished with his task, Store arched his back, preening. "Full house!"

Buchanan asked, "Like what?"

"Like what?"

"What kind of a full house?"

Store was incredulous. "You have a full house?"

Hagen said, "Just a minute. I've got a full house, too."

Now Store glared at Hempel, the dealer. "Kings full!"

Hagen said, "Beats my jacks full."

Buchanan said, "Hands sure are runnin' high. All the way up to aces full."

Store's voice was choked with a range of emotion. "I

don't know what is going on here." He stared first at Frey, then at Hempel. "I know something is very wrong."

Buchanan was putting his money in order. "You run Hagen out of the game, didn't you? You tapped him."

"I still do not like this."

"Nobody likes to lose," said Buchanan. "Mind if I stake Hagen, keep it five-handed?"

Store said coldly, "Do as you please."

Buchanan shoved a couple of hundred across to Hagen, who said, "Could be bad luck for you, stakin' a loser."

"I'll take that chance." Buchanan was watching Hempel. Out of the corner of his eye he saw the big deputy hold a card from the deck. He saw it stashed in the boot top n___ st him.

Th___ fa ce was coming to an end. The poker game designed to clean out Buchanan and Hagen—and probably kill th___ ___ad not been successful. They now, he knew, ___ ___ ___ __ke their play. The trick they had used before ___ __rked, therefore he believed they would try it ag___ He thought he saw a signal passed. Brannigan droppe___ hands below the bar. The tension became enormous.

Others had joined the belligerent Kelley in the street, ___ could hear the murmur beyond the locked doors. It would ___e up to those people, the citizens of Culebra, he tho___ They would decide the issue when the facts were ___ clear. There was no other law than the crooked depu___ represented. Which was no law at all.

He shuffled the deck, reading the edges of the car___ Hempel had held out an ace this time.

He said, "Maybe your luck will change, Tim," laying emphasis on every syllable, unlike his usual drawl.

Hagen understood, he felt. He looked at the girls. Addie was too close to the action. Flo remained at the piano. He fixed the position of everyone in the room, including Cook and the two Krags. He began to deal the cards, slowly watching Hempel. He was about to give himself the fifth pasteboard as Hempel reached toward his boot. Quicker than lightning, Buchanan swung his arm. He backhanded Hempel and sent the big man flying across the floor.

The ace fell out of Hempel's boot.

Buchanan seized the edge of the table. He flung it over. He drew his revolver.

"Just everybody hold it."

He had paid no attention to the rush of Cook and the Krags. Brannigan, he thought, was out of it. Addie was racing at Hempel, screaming, "Murderer!" Hagen had his gun out of the holster. Store and Frey were on the floor. It was all in a neat package.

Then Brannigan squealed in a high voice, "You drop your guns, you two."

"No dice," said Buchanan. "The gun's not loaded."

A shot nearly tore off his head. He stared. Brannigan had a big six-gun in each hand. He was saying, "I seen that dame. I seen what she did. I ain't no damn fool."

"Careful, Hagen," Buchanan said. "He's scared. He might kill one of the gals."

Hagen dropped his gun. Buchanan did the same. Store and Frey were getting to their feet. Hempel slapped Addie away from him.

Store said, "Arrest these men."

"Yeah. And then shoot us for tryin' to escape," said Buchanan. He was desperately trying to stall for time. He suddenly realized he had lost track of Flo Dockerty.

Store said, "Put them in jail."

Hempel and Frey started forward. A voice stopped them.

Flo Dockerty was standing on the piano bench. There was a gun in her hand. But what startled them out of their wits and froze them was her costume.

She was wearing the linen duster. Brannigan moved a hand and she fired at him. The bullet shattered the back mirror. Brannigan dropped his weapons.

"All right, you crooks," Flo said. "Your turn. Get those guns on the floor."

"Go get her," Store said wildly. "It's only a woman."

Hempel and Frey were unbuckling their belts. Frey said, "Guns don't care who shoots 'em. They ain't gonna murder us. So what's the big problem?"

Buchanan said, "The loot upstairs. The things we know. Any more questions?"

131

Hagen and Buchanan kicked the gun belts so that they were out of anyone's reach. Hagen took Brannigan's two weapons and tossed them, emptied, into a corner. Buchanan ran his hands over Store and found a derringer and a small pocket gun which he also slid into a corner. He started for Cook and the Krags when Addie came running.

He said, "No!" but she went on, sobbing, unaware of what she was doing, heading straight for Flo. Before anyone could stop her she was in the line of fire.

Cook bellowed, "Git 'em, tigers!"

Spike had his blackjack in his hand. Buchanan blocked the way to the discarded guns, but lacked his own Colt. Hagen looked lost, he was no fistfighter. Jasper Krag put up his hands and went for the ex-marshal.

Hempel, hot for vengeance, came rushing. Cook had a billy of his own. Flo was begging the addled Addie to get out of the way. Brannigan ran and wrested the gun from Flo, whereupon she kicked him so that he rolled, then pounced upon him. Again Addie, distracted out of her mind, interfered while trying to help.

The odds were just too big even for Buchanan. He had to grin—he could handle them two or three at a time but never all at once. He braced himself for the rush. Hagen went down under a swinging right hand from Jasper Krag, who now turned upon Buchanan.

Store made a break for where the weapons were piled. Buchanan left-handed the banker. He went upside down, squawking like an old hen, unaccustomed to physical combat.

Still it was too much. They were too many and now Hempel, his eyes red with his venomous hatred, reached back and unslung his Bowie knife.

It had been a bad gamble, thanks to unexpected turns and twists, Buchanan thought. He set himself for the end, hoping to get his hands on one of them, that he might again stall for time, any little bit of time that might prolong the battle.

The noise outside increased. But if the townsfolk broke in they would be confused, ignorant of the facts. There was really no hope, just a last stand against the odds.

The doors crashed open. A familiar voice cried, "There they is. Come on, Joe."

Coco Bean and Joe Konecke came roaring into the saloon. They headed straight for Cook and the Krags. There was blood in their eyes, they were swinging both hands.

"Coco! Welcome to the party!" Buchanan roared.

It was the wrong thing to do, he knew at once. Coco paused, startled, rolling his eyes. Spike jumped up and hit him in the head with his blackjack. Cook tried to follow up. Coco went back to the bar, staggering.

Hempel was coming with his Bowie. Frey, scuttling across the floor like a spider, was attempting to get at the guns. Addie, Flo, and Brannigan were a struggling heap of flying skirts and torn shirt as Brannigan tried to free himself and failed. Hagen was half-conscious, trying to get himself oriented. Konecke, single-minded, was belaboring Jasper Krag. And on the floor, Store was trying, in the midst of chaos, to stuff the scattered money into his pockets. At the door of the Silver Dollar, Kelley and the other ...smen stared, not knowing which side to take.

...uchanan sidestepped Hempel's rush. He kicked Frey ...ack and away from the guns. He went after Hempel and ...it him in the belly, then grabbed his right wrist. He twisted and got the big man off balance, then sent him whirling again.

Coco shook his head, recovering from astonishment at the fact of Buchanan's presence. He went back to work. He whacked Cook and dropped him to the floor. He picked up Spike and threw him, blackjack and all, over the bar so that he rattled among the bottles and scrambled amidst the glass shattered by Flo's bullet.

Flo sat astride Brannigan and flailed at him with her fists. Addie began to realize what was happening and kicked Brannigan in the head.

Frey made another try for the guns and Hagen, dazed, tackled him. Konecke continued to battle with Jasper. Coco went after Spike, plucked him from wreckage and battered his head against the bar until the little man lost consciousness.

Hempel swung with the Bowie knife, dizzy as a result of Buchanan's tactics. Store rose up, his hands full of the money from the toppled card table. The long knife described a circle and met Store's chest. The banker screamed in fear and agony and went down in a swelter of blood.

Hempel stared. Buchanan got to him, snatched away the knife and hit him with a curling right hook. Hempel went across the room standing up. Coco hit him again. Hempel went down.

Buchanan looked around. Hagen had a hammerlock on Frey. Someone outside was calling for Dr. Dudley. Cook was still on the floor. Brannigan was covering up to avoid being beaten by the girls. Konecke was disposing of Jasper Krag by knocking him cold. Coco and Konecke were descending upon the prone Cook with huge determination.

Buchanan walked across the room and found his six-shooter. He announced at the top of his lungs, "The party's over. Everybody pay heed."

Nobody gave him the least attention. He saw Dr. Dudley coming through the crowd with his bag. He decid~~~ was politic to start with the girls.

He hauled them off of Brannigan with great difficu~~ Brannigan came up fighting, his face scratched, his clo~~ ing in tatters. Buchanan tapped him with the muzzle of th~ Colt ~~d he lost interest in the proceedings.

~~ade~ and Konecke had turned out the pockets of Cook. C~~es ~~ad money and was counting it, with Konecke w~~~hing.

~~ "Steal from us, will you! Leavin' us to rot in that ole ~ail!" Coco was furious. "Run out with our money!"

Buchanan said, "So that's why you're here? You didn't come chasin' me again?"

Coco stopped yelling and beamed. "Like killin' two birds with one stone, huh? Got him . . . got you."

"I'll talk to you later. Don't let these birds get away," said Buchanan.

"Get away? I ain't likely to let 'em live," said Coco.

Dr. Dudley was working on Store. The wound was on the chest, high up near the shoulder, near the tip of the lung. Buchanan had a look at Hempel, who seemed to be sleeping soundly under the double ministration by Coco and himself. Hagen hurled Frey so that he fell across the

134

prone Cook. The little deputy's snake eyes sought Buchanan, blinked. Under the gun he stayed down, crouching, at bay.

Dr. Dudley said, "If I could put him on the bar it would help."

Buchanan motioned to Coco and Konecke. They picked up the banker and stretched him out among the spilled beer. The doctor continued to work on the wound.

Flo struggled out of the linen duster. She shrugged her gown back into place and came to Buchanan, hips swaying. "Guess I scared·'em for a minute, there," she said.

"Guess if it wasn't for Coco and Konecke you'd have got me killed dead," Buchanan told her.

"You'd have been dead anyway. They had you in a bind and don't you deny it."

"Okay . . . okay. Now I got to straighten this all out." Kelley and other citizens were gingerly entering the saloon. They stopped near the doorway, open mouthed and wide eyed.

Buchanan addressed them. "You know what's been goin' on in Culebra. Robberies and murders. Dani Dade, Dick Coverly, Sam Dade, Jody Teller. All connected one way or other to the bank, right?"

Kelley said, "Righto."

"Well I'm goin' to tell you the way I see it." He motioned to Flo and Addie to come forward. "I was told that Daniel Dade was carrying fifty-thousand dollars when he went off the cliff up on the Black Range. But we found that much and more, maybe, upstairs in a locked closet. The saddlebags had Daniel's initials on it. But I kept askin' where was he goin' with that much money. And why was he totin' it?"

"You got answers, boyo?" demanded Kelley. "I see you got the banker stabbed, the deputies disarmed. You and the ex-marshal, now, would ye be thinkin' of takin' over?"

Buchanan moved the Colt slightly. "For the moment, friend, for the moment we're takin' over. When I get finished, it'll be up to the town itself to take charge."

"Tell us the tale, then, Buchanan," said Kelley. He looked around for corroboration. "Is that right by all of yez?"

There was a chorus of assent. Buchanan went on.

"All right. Take my word, Daniel Dade was killed. And the money hidden in a locked closet in this building. Bank money."

A murmur went up from the crowd. Kelley asked, "Would that be our money, now?"

"It would—and is. Now I found out somethin' else. Walt Store was gamblin' on the stock exchange with bank money. He was losin'."

"With our money?"

"Young Sam Dade believed somethin' was wrong. He sent for auditors. They'll be here in a couple of days. So then young Sam got killed."

The murmur grew.

Buchanan said, "As to Dick Coverly, he knew where the money was hidden. He had meetings with Hempel and Frey. Then he got framed and killed right in this saloon."

"He was holdin' out a card!"

"He was not. Flo, here and me, we both knew he wasn't. Hempel and Frey have been tryin to kill me or run me outa town because they knew he was framed—and because I was gettin' closer to 'em."

"The deputies are in it?" demanded Kelley, his neck swelling. "Those spalpeens?"

"The same," said Buchanan. "My friend Jody Teller was in on enough of it because he was afraid the bank would close and he'd lose everything he owned. Somewhere along the line—I believe it was when they wanted to kill me—he balked. He got killed."

Frey cried, "A pack o' lies. Nobody'll believe such a pack o' lies."

"Shut up an' listen, you dirty little divvil," said Kelley. "I've me eye on you for a long time. The Apache Mine wants to know who sent the message delayin' that payroll on the very day the bank was robbed."

"I was gettin' to that," said Buchanan. "Linen dusters. Found a bit of cloth torn from one out at the deserted farmhouse the bank didn't try to rent out. Found the one you see which Flo Dockery has here. They probably wore 'em when they killed Dan'l Dade. We found less'n a thousand on Sandy Folger, but Walt Store claimed the loss was in the big numbers. Walt Store was coverin' his losses every way he could. He brought in Hempel and Frey and tried to make a figurehead outa Tim Hagen. He twisted and turned and stole and lied and had four men killed."

Dr. Dudley interposed. "He'll live to answer questions. Maybe not much more'n that."

"And if he talks he'll hang Hempel and Frey," said Buchanan. "A knife to cut papers from Daniel Dade's coat pocket—Hempel carries the big knife. Quick gun and quick escape after Sam and Jody Teller were killed— Frey's the gunner who moves like a rattler."

"You can't prove nothin'," Frey screamed at him.

"He's right," said Kelley. "Ye got to have the proof."

Buchanan surveyed the crew, landed on Jasper Krag as a weak vessel. He asked, "Who brought you here, Jasper?"

"I dunno. Cook said to come."

"Spike?"

"Ye'll git nothin' from me but the back o' me hand." The little man spat out the words.

"Cook?"

"I ain't talkin'."

"Well, that might get you hanged. Because the truth will out. The auditors will find what happened to the bank money. We happen to have proof Store gambled it away."

"You got nothin'." It was Frey again. "You're makin' bad guesses is all."

There was a disturbance among the citizens of Culebra. Jackson, the telegrapher, pushed his way to the foreground. His bald head shone in the light.

'Mr. Buchanan is right. I've got the proof. I want that money back in the bank. I got the telegrams Store sent to the brokers in San Francisco."

Frey said, "I'll kill you . . ." He started forward and Buchanan slapped him back to where Hagen, his revolver recovered, held him.

Cook wiped his florid face. "Wait, I'll tell you. Store knew us from a few deals on fights and such. He sent for me, so we come here after the sheriff rousted us. But I don't know nothin' about any killin's. Rough work is us, not killin'."

137

"And what about Spike fakin' it at the bank robbery? Folger, Hempel, Frey—and Spike to bring the linen duster and the loot over here. Brannigan, you want to talk?"

Brannigan said, "I didn't kill nobody. I put the money in saddlebags like they told me, sure. When Addie was drinkin'. But no killin', not me, no sir."

"All so innocent," said Buchanan. "All helpin' a man to steal a town but still like the newborn babe. Are you satisfied, Kelley?"

Dr. Dudley spoke again, coming from the bar. "I'll answer. You see, people forget I'm a selectman. Guess I'm too busy to be very active. But I am one. I hereby dismiss Hempel and Frey to be held for questioning in the jail. I also restore Tim Hagen as marshal. I must also ask help in removing Mr. Store to my office, where I can watch over him and ease his last hours. I would request that a committee of citizens led by Mr. Kelley sit with me in case Mr. Store wishes to talk before he dies." He looked at Buchanan. "I would wish also that you would resume your position in the Silver Dollar until matters can be straightened out."

Buchanan said, "You better put 'em all in jail."

"Oh, my yes," said Dr. Dudley. "All of them. They must be given the chance to make statements. I will call for the circuit judge to hold a session of court. Oh, my yes."

Buchanan said, "Fine. Then my work is done. You can get someone to take over the Silver Dollar. Maybe Flo Dockerty. She does a great job, believe me."

"Not on your life," said Flo. "I've got other plans."

She beamed upon Buchanan. He winced. Hagen rounded up his prisoners. Hempel was still groggy; Frey was cursing Buchanan; the Krags were sullen, and Cook frightened. They all marched to the jailhouse.

Dr. Dudley said, "I'll talk to you later, Mr. Buchanan. I believe the town owes you a lot."

"Two thousand dollars," said Flo.

"Two thousand dollars?"

"What Sam Dade, representing the bank, offered if we'd get to the bottom of it all. Soon as one of 'em confesses— and Store'll squawk, he's no hero. Plus the money on the floor, there, and what he picked up from the poker table. That's our money."

Buchanan said, "Now, just a minute." Then he shut up. He had other worries. Coco was waiting to get in his two cents worth.

Chapter Ten

The light was low in the room where Walt Store lay dying. He had hung on for days, until the auditors had come to town and discovered his chicanery with the bank accounts and checked them with the coded telegrams preserved by Jackson. Now, his life ebbing, he was reconciled to defeat.

He spoke softly and clearly so that Buchanan, Dr. Dudley and one of the auditors, a man named Robinson, could hear. "Daniel was not carrying fifty thousand dollars. thought he was going to meet me to talk over bank los he did not understand. Oh, we'd made some wrong inv ments together. I thought I could recoup in mining stock. lost." His voice failed and Dr. Dudley wiped his lips with a damp cloth.

He resumed. "Hempel and Frey. They got rid of Daniel for me. They got rid of everyone who seemed to get in our way. Excepting Buchanan." He smiled faintly, then went on. "It got so I knew I couldn't save the bank. I thought to go elsewhere, change my identity and begin again. After Daniel, Coverly had to be eliminated because he knew too much. Jody Teller began to back down and Frey shot him. We staged the robbery to clean the bank out altogether and give me time to make arrangements—and to get rid of Sam. Sorry about Sam, I liked the young man."

Again he stopped. Now Dr. Dudley shook his head. But Store rallied.

"Hempel took a shot at Buchanan early in the game, when he was seen riding the deserted farm and ranch. It was always Buchanan. I thought to enlist him but realized it was no use. I tried to keep him where we could watch him . . . brought in Cook and the Krags to use as tools . . .

140

Brannigan . . . too many cooks spoil the broth, they say. Desperation . . . I hope none of you gentlemen know such desperation. . . ."

He closed his eyes. He was wan and wasted. Probably a good man once, Buchanan thought, like so many others. Chasing the dollar, always after money and power. It had brought down many a better man.

Dr. Dudley said, "He's gone. It was a deathbed confession. I believe we can hang Hempel and Frey."

"I doubt it," said Robinson. "Prison, yes. Hanging—that's another matter under territorial law. However, the judge is here now. The courts will decide."

Buchanan felt hemmed in. He would have been gone before now had he not been wanted as a witness. He looked at the dead man on the bed. He shrugged and walked out and went down the street to the Silver Dollar.

Flo awaited him at a table in the rear. Business was good, the town was rejuvenated by the news that the bank was again sound. The big man, Kelley, had decided to give up laboring in the mines and take over as bartender. Flo and Buchanan awaited the new manager recommended by the auditors, due in from Silver City. He told Flo what had happened.

"Just like you said." She smiled upon him.

"Jackson pinned it all down. Without the records to prove where the money went—we didn't ever have real proof of anything. Store was a clever man."

"And now he's a clever corpse."

"Yeah. Well, where's Addie?"

"Carryin' a hot meal to Tim Hagen at the jail."

"Bless them."

She said, "Oh-oh. Here comes Coco and friend."

The black fighter and the silent fighter came and sat down at the table. They had their stake back, but little more. They were training every day, boxing each other in the livery stable that had belonged to Jody Teller. They were restless, although Konecke, as usual, said nothing.

Coco said to Buchanan, "Seems like least you could do was come to the stable and fight me. You ain't got no wound to bellyache about this time."

"I been busy," Buchanan explained. "We got to get

141

those fellas tried and convicted. I can't be messin' around."

"Sooner or later I'm gonna whup you." Coco held up an iron fist. "Sooner or later."

Flo cried, "What? What's that you say?"

"Just a notion Coco's got," Buchanan hastily explained. "He's been harpin' on it for some time now."

"You couldn't whip Buchanan with a gun and a club, one in each hand," she told Coco. "You crazy or somethin'?"

Coco said, "You seen me fight. You know I kin do it."

"I saw Buchanan fight, too," she said. "Whooooeee!"

Buchanan said, "Flo, will you hush up? Now, I've got an idea."

"You gonna fight me?" demanded Coco.

"Well, not quite. Not yet."

"Yawl see? If he ain't got some wound from some doggone gun—how I hates guns—he got some other excuse."

"Well, you boys need money." Further inspiration descended upon Buchanan. "Flo, you listen to this. We can finance this and make a mint for us all."

"I'm not financin' anything. I got my money socked away." They had collected from the bank, thanks to Dr. Dudley.

"This can't miss." The idea grew in his mind. "Tomorrow's the trial. Now you know that people from all over the country'll be here for that. People with money to spend. Outside the Silver Dollar, what's to spend it on? So . . . we promote a boxin' match."

"You an' me!" said Coco, eyes shining.

"Now, how could we do that, me testifyin' and everything? No, betwixt you and Joe, here."

"Hey, that might work," cried Flo.

"Sure. And I'll pay for banners and dodgers and you can promote it," Buchanan said. "A lady promoter, now that'll get 'em comin' and goin'."

"Me, a fight promoter?" But light was in her eyes.

"Who dressed like a boy to get herself onto the barge when Coco fought Joe?"

She was growing excited. "I could get in the ring and announce 'em and all."

142

"Right," said Buchanan.

Coco said, "I got a better idea. Me and Joe fight. Then we tell 'em Buchanan will fight the winner. After the trial and all."

"Great!" said Flo. "How about that?"

Buchanan crossed his fingers behind his back. "Now that might solve the whole thing. Make Coco happy and all."

"Then we'll do it. Won't we, Joe?"

Konecke, never a man to waste words, nodded.

Flo said, "Hey! You know what would really draw 'em in? We could raise the price to the sky?"

"What?"

"If you and me got married in the ring after the fight!"

"Oh, no," said Buchanan. "If I get married ever, it'll be in church like decent people."

"It would sure make money," Flo said. "Oh, well, wherever you want is all right with me, long as we get married."

"Uh—yeah," said Buchanan. "Well, I got to see the printer and all. Get it started." He stood up and regarded them fondly. "It sure is good to be among friends. So long for now."

He dutifully went to the printer, gave him some copy for dodgers, and then he went to where the judge was sitting in the lobby of the hotel, an elderly man named Hotchkiss.

He said, "Judge, I heard of such a thing as a deposition. Like when a man's got important business outta town or somethin' and can't be in court."

"That's right. There is such a thing."

"Well, now Store's dead and has confessed and I ain't got any real, simon-pure evidence and people were around when the loot was discovered and all, could I make a deposition?"

"You might see the prosecutor. He's in Room 201 this moment. Sorry you have to leave, Mr. Buchanan. I've heard a lot about you."

"Thank you, sir," said Buchanan.

An hour later he was packed. He sneaked out of the

hotel and went to Teller's stable. He saddled Nightshade, and threw his saddlebags and bedroll into place. He mounted and rode toward the Black Range.

Marriage, he thought. Worse, far, far worse than fighting Coco Bean. She was a cute little old gal and all that. But marriage? Never!